Dragon Engaged
Copyright © 2019 by Viola Grace
ISBN: 978-1-987969-60-3

©Cover art by Angela Waters

Published by Viola Grace

Look for me online at violagrace.com, Sea to Sky Books, Amazon, Smashwords, Kobo, B&N, and other eBook sellers.

Other Books in This Series

The Bastard Dragon
Dragon Astray

Dragon Engaged
The Covert Dragons Book 3

By

Viola Grace

Chapter One

Trin twirled slowly in the chair. "This is so boring!"

Meadra was sitting and knitting in the chair. "You are very good at languages."

"My dragon is good at it. I am just good at knowing when it is time to let her talk." Trin sat up and finished the paperwork for Apraxa's import business.

"What would you be doing in the capitol?"

"Probably playing with Creata's baby or tormenting Brenner and Niida. Or tormenting Brommin. That is a new hobby." She chuckled.

"When can we leave Breaker City?"

Trin spun the chair again. "Two more days."

Meadra perked up. "That soon?"

"Yup. We have your gown, my gown is waiting for me, so we just have to kill forty-eight hours, and we can get on Ystine and drive home."

Meadra swallowed. "Are you sure that you don't mind me staying with you?"

"You will be staying with the dragons. They will be happy to have you." Trin stopped spinning and got up to collapse on the sofa. "And, of course, you should be with me. You are my aunt or mother or aunty-mom."

Meadra blushed and kept knitting.

"That sounds silly."

"This situation isn't normal, so silly makes it feel better." Trin chuckled and then paused. "Are you worried?"

"About what?"

"About your family coming for you."

"*Our* family, and no. Not with you here. You are way scarier than they are." Meadra smiled and kept working.

Trin was restless. She may have asked the question about Meadra's family coming for her, but it was deadly serious. Her aunt was an asset that they weren't going to part with. Hiding her away from the capitol was a measure of desperation. It also felt right. Apraxa needing someone to mind the store while she was gone had also seemed to be weirdly coincidental.

So, now, she just needed to check in

on her gown, and she and Meadra could head home for the ball. The next two days were going to crawl by.

Trin tapped her fingers together and thought, perking up slightly. "Do you want to go for a walk?"

Meadra smiled. "A walk?"

"Yes. There is a temple a few blocks over that should be alive with light tonight."

Trin smiled as her aunt put her knitting away.

"Is it safe?"

"No, but it is better than being cooped up here. You don't have to come with me. I can set all the alarms." Trin got to her feet and stretched.

"I am coming. Is it a festival?"

"I think it is the Blood Moon Festival. There is a species celebrating something just about every week here. The temples are always busy. I am just going to go change. Back in a minute."

Trin headed to her guestroom and went through her clothing. She settled on the black bodysuit with the silver-piped dress overtop. Her knives were strapped to her thighs, and flat batons were tied to her inner forearms under the sleeves of the dress. The belt that she put on held the whole outfit together and also contained her wallet and some small blades in the leather. Being armed at a festival was tacky, but she would just leave a large donation at the temple.

She pinned her hair up into a loose fall, checked her reflection, and put her boots on. She wanted to have fun, but she was practical. There was a bounty on her head and on Meadra's. The social niceties could be had, but adaptation had to occur, or stupidity could cost them their lives or freedom. She would wear knives into a temple.

Sighing, Trin returned to the living area, and she grinned when Meadra was nowhere to be found. Her aunt was almost as fashion hungry as she was and was now finally able to indulge.

"Is this all right?" Meadra came in and did a slow turn. Her outfit was dark red and black. It looked lovely on her and fit her as if it had been made for her. It was part of her new wardrobe and her first non-hand-me-down.

"It is very appropriate. Shall we?"

Having her aunt giggling and clapping as they left the warehouse helped her mood. She remained on alert, but she started to see the beauty and excitement that worry had blinded her to.

At first, the streets near the warehouse were empty, but as they got closer to the temple, other folk in finery joined them on the path.

Trin's smile came easier as they entered the temple grounds where food stalls had been set up, and games were being played. The blood moon was enormous, but it hadn't yet reached its zenith. They had two hours to play before the howling of the wolf shifters and thrashing of the shark shifters took over the night. It would not be particularly safe at that point.

"Trin! I mean, Mistress Lem, how nice to see you!" She knew that voice. Hector was leading the pack of his brothers with his wife and three little ones in the group.

Apraxa's brothers were focused on them, and Trin grinned. "Thank you for the greeting. I haven't been in Breaker City for any of the festivals before."

Hector's wife stepped forward. "I don't believe we have met."

"We have not, Kohasi, though your husband spoke of nothing else when Apraxa and I meet in the family diner. I hope your children have enjoyed the gifts I sent for their naming days."

The woman blinked, and a slow smile spread across her face. "You are Mistress Lem."

"Trin, please. I see that the whole family is here."

Kohasi grinned. "Everyone except for Apraxa. She has her hands full."

Trin fought a smirk. "Yes, well, hopefully, she is making progress."

She suddenly realized that there was a very curious female in the vicinity. "Kohasi, this is my aunt, Meadra. Meadra, this is Hector's wife, Kohasi."

Meadra reached for Kohasi's hand, and she murmured, "Bright greetings, mother of Torin, Mekker, and Albert."

Kohasi blushed, and Hector grinned.

Trin inclined her head. "My family takes children very seriously."

Troy and Pollux cleared their throats in unison.

Troy said, "Well, as Hector is occupied with his family, would you ladies like a tour of the temple grounds?"

Kohasi chuckled. "Don't let us slow you down."

Trin shrugged. "Sure. I would like to pay my respects to the temple first, and I don't want Meadra out of my sight, so keep that in mind. If I lose her, you lose limbs."

The two brothers nodded in agreement. "We are good with that."

Pollux walked up to Meadra and offered his arm, Troy did the same to Trin. They walked slightly ahead of the others, and he said in a grand voice, "Welcome to the Blood Moon Festival."

She grinned and inclined her head. "Thank you."

They walked past booths that would tell the past, present, and future, kiosks full of snacks that smelled and looked like they contained a week of calories, and finally, they reached the temple in a small oasis of decorum.

"Keep an eye on Meadra; I need to pay my respects."

The two sharks turned to their prey,

and Meadra smiled pleasantly. "So, are you two seeing anyone?"

Trin chuckled and headed inside the temple, noting the three different altars that were carefully tended and garlanded with flowers.

Trin paid her respects to the wolf god and the shark god, but the goddess of the land was covered in flowers and was draped in plain green silk. Trin took a few hundred dollars, and she slipped it into the donation slots, thought about what she wanted, clapped three times, bowed, and clapped again.

When she straightened, she could swear that the goddess of the temple winked at her. She inclined her head in return and left to find Meadra and the sharks.

A quick glance didn't turn up her friends and family, so she used her dragon's senses to seek Meadra out. Blood called to blood in this case.

There. A flicker at the edge of the grounds where the boys had sworn not to go. Trin moved as swiftly as she could with her determination strong and her fighting brain coming online.

She ran into Kohasi, and the woman stopped her. "What is wrong?"

"The boys are leaving the grounds with my aunt. This is not good, and they would not have done it on their own."

Kohasi nodded and glanced around. "You find them; I will let Hector know."

Trin nodded and continued to track Meadra. She moved swiftly. The crowd parted when they saw her coming. Those who weren't looking were yanked out of her way by those who were facing her.

She caught the scent of another drag-on and the dark whiff of human magic. Things were far more complicated than Trin had been hoping. Pity, it had looked to be a very pleasant evening.

Chapter Two

$\mathcal{T}$rin flexed her wrists as she closed in on the group that was trying hard not to incur notice. She thought that was a good idea and blurred herself into invisibility.

The sharks each had a gun aimed at their backs, and Meadra was being held between two men who had stiffly pleasant expressions on their faces. Trin grinned and thought to herself, *That is about to change.*

There was another member of their party nearby, but she wanted to get the boys free of the threat, or Apraxa would never forgive her.

She moved toward the men with the guns, flicked her batons out, and struck quickly, hearing the crack of their wrists as the guns were forced down.

"Take care of them," Trin muttered as she moved toward the men who had picked Meadra up and were hauling her bodily toward the street.

It was difficult to do while unseen, but she extended her wings and jumped up and over the trio, pulling knives and stabbing each of the men in the shoulder when Meadra collided with her.

She flashed back to visible as the men reeled back, and she pulled Meadra away from her abductors.

A slow clapping sound made her turn slightly to put herself between Meadra and the noise.

"Who are you, mage?"

The mage walked forward, and while he had devastatingly good looks, there was a sneer in his expression that Trin didn't care for.

"I am sorry to inconvenience you, but the project is coming with me."

Meadra gasped.

"No, she isn't. She is my guest, she is my kin, and she is staying with me."

The two men who had had a grip on Meadra backed off when the mage fired up his hands with power.

"Meadra, stay behind me and get ready to hang on."

The mage snorted. "You can't carry anyone in that form. I am amazed you could move at all with those enormous encumbrances."

She inclined her head and didn't respond. He fired one shot after another, and she twisted, catching and scooping the power with her wings, flinging it back in a weirdly smooth move that her dragon engaged in while roaring wilding in her mind.

The mage was struck and flew up and back several dozen metres. He wouldn't be doing anything else tonight.

Trin saw a crowd of sharks bringing up the rear with Kohasi at their head.

Kohasi nodded. "Go, we will take care of the leftovers."

Trin smiled. "Thank you. I just need to retrieve something."

She walked toward the two men wearing her knives and jerked the implements out while the men screamed. The sharks surrounded them, and Trin returned to Meadra. "Come along, Aunt."

She scooped Meadra up and launched skyward, flying in a wide loop before she settled back into invisibility and returning to Apraxa's home.

She landed on the roof and resumed her visibility. "Well, that was less fun than I had hoped."

Meadra nodded, and then, her lower lip wobbled, a fat tear made its way down her cheek. "They said they would kill you or the sharks if I cried out."

"It's fine. We are all fine, and they all need medical help, especially that mage. Ouch."

Meadra sniffled as they walked toward the door. "I know. That was amazing. How did you do that?"

Trin chuckled. "I have no idea. The

dragon knows what she can do, but she only tells me when I express a need."

Meadra nodded as they entered the security door. "Do you think that I have a dragon in me?"

"I am pretty sure you do, but what kind it is, is up for grabs."

Meadra touched her arm. "Can you bring her out?"

Trin's dragon perked up.

Trin shook her head. "I would like to do it at the guildhall in the Wheel. That way, if things go wrong, there are other dragon females around to help."

Meadra nodded. "That sounds good."

"They will insist on keeping you close to them, but that is the best place to be safe."

Her aunt paused as they entered the

main living space. "If it is so safe, why are you here instead of there?"

"I would have left anyway. I had to find out where my mother came from." Trin gave her a hug. "I was very worried tonight."

"Me too, but you just looked angry."

Trin backed up and wrinkled her nose. "Angry and worried look sort of the same on me. Either way, unless I say otherwise when you see that face, hold very still."

Meadra laughed.

Apraxa's voice sounded from the living space. "I am curious. Tell me what has been going on."

Trin stepped around the last barrier and looked at Apraxa as she sat on the couch with a mug of tea next to her. "What are you doing home?"

Apraxa was sporting a claw mark and a black eye but looked otherwise fine. "My mother decided that my presence was no longer desirable, so I came home."

Trin nodded, but Meadra stared. "She hit you?"

Apraxa quirked her lips. "She did."

"What did you do?"

"I hit her back. Then, I apologized to my grandparents and got the hell out of there before I was tempted to do anything foolish."

Trin had to ask, "What about the guy?"

Apraxa winced. "It got complicated, even for an arrangement. He wanted possession of my businesses, and I told him to fuck off."

"Oh. That is understandable." Trin

got it. If Brommin tried to interfere in her business in the future, he was going to feel the back and front of her hand.

"Yeah, well, when I started it in the middle of the court, he got a little huffy, and his family had to haul him off before he got arrested." She finished her tea. "I left shortly after that."

Trin grinned. "How shortly?"

"About five minutes. I made my bows to the court and got back in the water. It was a fun visit with my mother's family, but I prefer it back here in Breaker City. Oh, that said, can I come with you to the capitol? I have a funny feeling that this place isn't going to be safe for me in a few days."

Meadra looked at Trin, and they laughed. Trin held up her hand. "Let me just check on my gown, and we can go.

Did we want to drive or fly?"

Apraxa waited until she was walking away and then said, "Don't you have a gown waiting in the capitol?"

"I didn't really have time, and I am not sure that Mirbella had time to finish it." A call could confirm it, but Trin felt a little bit guilty about all the weird work that had already been given to the seamstress.

Apraxa propped her elbow on the arm of the chair and used her fist to support her head. "I called earlier and gave her my measurements. She said she could provide me with a shifting gown now that yours was taken care of."

Trin paused and turned around. "So, you already had it figured out."

"I know about the festival. I guessed

you would want to leave as soon as possible." Apraxa looked at Meadra. "Are you all right?"

Meadra nodded, and her chin wobbled for a moment before she took a deep breath. "Yes. I am fine, and none of ours got hurt. Your brothers are fine."

Apraxa nodded and waved that away. "They were your guards, they should have been paying attention. That said, I am glad they are fine. I can assure you that the attackers are not."

Trin smiled. "I am glad it was on their terms and not mine."

"They learned a bit about sharks, and the sharks learned what happens when you eat mage blood. My brothers are going to be jumping anything with breasts for a few days. Best that we get Meadra out of town. Can you fly us?"

Meadra got an excited gleam to her eyes. "I will go pack for both of us. What will you do with Ystine?"

Trin smiled. "I will put her in the yard and pick her up as I fly. I will call Creata and ask her if we can land at her house."

Apraxa wrinkled her nose. "I suppose I should make an appointment to register with the guild as well."

"That might be a good idea if you are going to attend the ball." Trin grinned. Meadra had left the room and was probably packing frantically.

"Probably. I have the family invitation, so I can get in under that, but the registration will mean I can take a pick if I like one of the guys on offer." Apraxa winked.

Trin winced. If Apraxa was engaged,

there was a sense of possession in play. She was thinking of teaching her male a lesson, and that wasn't a good thing.

"Right. Well, if you can get what you need, I will call Creata and get Ystine into the forecourt. We can be out of here in an hour."

"Righto. I will get my bag."

Trin blinked at the weird turn of the evening, and she put in a call to Creata.

"Trin? Are you all right?" It had become her standard greeting when Trin called.

"I am fine. I am coming home. Can we land at your place tonight?"

"Of course. I will have two rooms readied."

"Could you make it three? I am bringing Apraxa along as well."

Creata chuckled. *"Excellent. We will*

have a sleepover. The baby will love it."

"Okay. We will fly out in an hour, and I will drop Ystine first. You can check on your other baby." Trin laughed.

"I will have a snack waiting and fire up the security system."

"See you soon."

The call ended, and Trin looked around. *Right, time to leave the hideaway.*

Trin was wearing one of her shifting outfits as she stood on the roof. "Once I shift, I won't be able to talk, but I can hear you. Get the stuff onto my back and strapped down as quick as you can then get in place. Once everything is set, I will take off and grab Ystine. From there, it is straight to the capitol. Got it?"

Meadra nodded, her hands on her

bags and ready to throw. "Got it."

Apraxa nodded. "Got it. The cargo webbing is ready. When you shift, we move."

Trin looked at the two women who were bundled up for a cold night. She was going to have to fly high to maximize her invisibility, so they were going to get chilled.

Trin made sure everything was ready, and she shifted, balancing over the bearing walls of the home beneath her.

Apraxa moved quickly, and Meadra started to hurl the luggage upward with the skill of a farm girl.

Less than a minute after they had started, Meadra was attaching the cargo strap under Trin's belly and around her neck. She barely felt anything, as if they were made of dandelion fluff.

When Apraxa finished settling everything, she said, "We are good to go."

Trin nodded and stretched her wings. She rose carefully from her crouch and walked to the edge of the warehouse, flaring her full wingspan until there was air caressing every part of her. A light hop sent her sailing down, and she reached out her hind claws and caught Ystine, carrying her carefully as her wings began to beat.

The moment she had her velo, she went invisible, and her wings scooped vast volumes of air behind her and under her. Breaker City grew smaller and smaller as she climbed, and when she had the altitude she wanted, she went visible and hid in the clouds. The trip to the capitol would take hours, and she needed to put on as much speed as she could without intercepting any other aerial passenger vessels.

She kept her senses trained on her riders, but they seemed fine. This long stretch as herself was rather freeing. No panic, no emergencies, just flying home to be with friends and her mate.

Hmm. The thought of her mate was filling her mind, and it was welcome. Brommin was going to be hers in front of witnesses, or she would beat any female who got between them.

Trin wanted her bookish assassin in her arm as fast as she could manage it. If his father weren't the senator ruling all of the northern continents, it would not be such a huge deal.

Family ties could be cumbersome, but she was willing to learn how to manage them.

Chapter Three

She kept her invisibility up until she was fifty feet from the ground. With care, she set Ystine down near the garage, and from there, she came to a loping stop in the middle of the expansive yard.

Creata came out of the house with the baby on her shoulder. Trin shifted from dragon to woman, shucking out of her harness and passengers in one move.

Apraxa and Meadra went tumbling across the rich lawn, landing at the feet of their hostess.

Trin sauntered across the grass and

reached out her hands. "She has gotten so big! And you are looking so happy!"

She hugged her friend first, and then, she kidnapped the baby for a blast of air pressed against the chubby cheek.

Creata grinned. "You hardly ever do that to me anymore."

"You started fighting back." Trin eased the baby onto her shoulder and patted her back.

"Well, it got a little silly at my wedding."

"You started it." Trin chuckled. "Oh, I have introductions to make. Creata Tal, this is my friend Apraxa and my aunt, Meadra."

Creata was surprised. "Meadra, you look just like Trin, well, close enough to be sisters. I mean, Trin told me, but this is still amazing."

Apraxa nodded. "It has to be seen to be believed. Who knew that Trin wasn't one of a kind? It is good to see you in person, Creata. I have enjoyed chatting with Ystine, but hearing my own voice does get a little wearing."

Trin smirked. "I had my suspicions that the novelty would wear off for you."

Creata grinned. "I think she sounds great. Her voice is very soothing, like sleeping next to rushing waves."

Trin rolled her eyes. The baby snuffled and rubbed her face against Trin's shoulder. There was a little drool involved, but that was the least evil that tiny Amesthet could unleash.

Creata called out, "Ystine, can you head to the garage? I will do an overhaul in the morning."

"Yes, Creata. It will be nice to be out of the clutches of a madwoman for a while."

Trin grinned. "Thanks for the compliment, Ystine."

Creata sighed and walked across the yard in her ruffled robe and silky nightgown. She escorted the velocipede into the camouflaged workshop, and then, she came back to those waiting for her.

"All right. Give her back."

Trin turned away from Creata, letting the baby look at her mom. "Give who back?"

"Esty. Give her back, it is time for her feeding. Ladies, shall we return to the house?"

Trin pouted. "Can I hold her while we walk?"

"Fine, but if she cries and I start dripping milk, I am blaming you."

A child had never been passed over that quickly in the history of dragons and lions.

Creata laughed softly and took her daughter back.

The sight of the two together was a relief for Trin. Time and a therapist had healed a lot of wounds.

"Before you ask, there was an emergency council tonight, so Vasic is at the Wheel."

Trin was a little disappointed. It looked like Brommin was going to be busy.

Creata walked through the garden door that a maid was holding open. She carried her child through the house and into a sitting room.

Trin glanced behind her, and her

travel companions were right behind her.

They all settled around Creata as she arranged herself to feed her daughter. "I will be happy when she can make it through the night, but since we were going to be up anyway, I am glad the timing matched up."

"I live to serve." Trin winked and sat back with a groan.

Meadra was looking around in shock. "Is this a palace?"

Creata smiled. "No, it is a mansion. It belongs to my husband's family. We only have three servants on duty at any given time and two gardeners. I do love the gardens."

Apraxa nodded, and she slowly slumped into an upright sleeping posture.

Creata was alarmed. "Is she all right?"

Trin nodded. "She's fine, just tired. I am pretty sure that she swam most of the Atlantic today."

Meadra yawned.

Creata smiled. "Mina can show you to your bed if you can help Apraxa up the steps."

Meadra looked at the maid who was next to the doorway, and she nodded. "I will get her."

Trin watched in amazement as her aunt picked up Apraxa and flipped her over her shoulder. While upside-down, Apraxa began to snore with enthusiasm.

The baby snuffled but calmed when the audible disturbance moved out of her range.

Trin looked at Creata and shook her

head. "Wow. I had no idea she had it in her."

Creata chuckled. "Neither did I. She seems so ladylike."

"Yes, well, looks can be deceiving. So, how are you really getting on?"

"It has only been a few weeks."

"I know, but it feels like longer. Little Esty is already so big."

Creata smiled. "Brommin was here this afternoon. He just came by to check on us with Vasic being stuck on administrative duty."

Trin felt her cheeks getting a little warm. "Was he?"

"He asked how you were doing. Really doing. Apparently, he doesn't trust your reports."

"Well, I have tried to be direct, but sometimes, it isn't easy. Telling him that

Apraxa was a dragon was a little tense. He never really unclenched after that." She twisted her mouth.

"Are you ready for the ball?"

"Not quite yet. I still need to check in with Mirbella."

Creata smiled. "She will be here in the morning. Apraxa called her."

There was a shy look in her eyes as she looked at Trin. "It is nice having visitors. It is sort of like a sleepover."

"I am glad you are enjoying it. As long as we don't put you in danger, we will stay here and lie low."

Creata gave her a sly look. "You are going to go visit him."

"Of course not. That would be inappropriate." Trin chuckled. "I have a great respect for decorum; I just can't seem to manage it."

"Oh, it is good to have you home. I feel better when you are here."

"I feel better, too. For better or worse, this is home. Now, I just need to take out the assassins that have been tracking me, and I will be fine."

"Don't put yourself in harm's way."

"I am already there. I am just going to try and injure all those who would take a shot."

Creata frowned. "You are suddenly very cocky for someone whose favourite accomplishment was drawing a happy face in the foam on her coffee."

"I have learned a few things about my dragon. She's a lot more durable than I first thought, and I am going to get use out of that." She paused. "I do need to get more knives, though."

"Are you still getting them from

Takka?"

"I hope so. Is she all right?"

"The last time I heard from her, she was doing great. I needed some parts for Ystine, and you know she does some of the best machining in the city."

"I do know that, and that is why I am going to go to her place tomorrow."

"Today."

Trin nodded in agreement and held up her index finger. "Right. That one."

"Trin, are you okay? You seem a little punchy, well, more than normal."

"I am fine. Well, a little giddy. The transformation does that to me. It is still fairly new."

Creata chuckled. "You are lying, but it is all right. You're in the north guest room, and there is a balcony. You can take off and land from there."

"So, you know that I have mastered all the forms?"

"Oh, I expect nothing less from you. Now, go. I want you back before I have to do the next feeding. I will need a situation report."

Trin laughed and got up to press a kiss to Creata's forehead. "I promise not to skip the details. Be back before dawn."

"Good. Details are what I live for now that I am stuck here and in my lab. Esty is coming along really well. She can tell the difference between wires already."

Trin grinned and winked, heading out of the living area and up the steps. Her room's door was open, and the bed was turned down. It was like being in a high-class hotel.

She closed her door and locked it before crossing the room to the balcony doors and opening them to the night air. Her dragon was urging her to her destination, so she concealed herself on the way through the doors and took off when her wings had filled out enough to support her weight.

It was a different feeling to fly from wings positioned in a human body. Her dragon form was almost liquid in the air, but her arms and legs were constantly tugging her off balance. She flew to the centre of the city and circled the tower before locating the scent that she was looking for. There were a lot of very powerful dragons in the tower right now. More than normal.

It seemed that with the ball so close, guests were arriving. Dragons from every corner of the globe were invited if they were single. The eligible men would gather, and the eligible women would choose. There were always more men than women, so it meant that the odds were better if you had breasts.

There! Her dragon focused on the long windows in question, and when she reached out, she peeled them open and stepped into Brommin's quarters.

He wasn't sleeping, he was standing next to his desk, and he was bare to the waist. "Are you coming in, Trin?"

She folded her wings behind her and let her concealment fade. "How did you know?"

He walked up to her and ran his hands down her arms. "There is no other invisible dragon in the country."

She would have replied, but his kiss

was wild, strong, and headily seductive.

His hand held the back of her head, and she slid her hands across the fascinatingly hot and smooth skin of his chest. The wild flapping in her mind was her highly excited dragon beating out any thoughts of slowing down.

His arms pulled her in and stroked the folds of her wings while he covered her lips with short, biting kisses.

His frenzy was a little startling, but Trin was all for it. He pulled back, and she dug her nails into his chest. She whispered, "Don't go."

Brommin slowly leaned back, but he kept her in his arms. "I have missed you."

Her lips felt a little swollen. "I can tell. How are your parents?"

"That is an odd question after the

kiss, but my mother is fine, and my father is as he ever was, serious and nervous about the plans for the ball."

Her palms were flat on his chest, and her dragon was doing a slow happy roll in her mind.

"Why did you come, Trin?"

"I missed you." She wrinkled her nose. "Too trite?"

"No, just right. Where are you staying?"

"Creata's. I brought guests with me."

"Dragons?" He raised his brows.

"Yes. Apraxa and Meadra. We are going to see if we can get Meadra to shift tomorrow. If she does, she can attend the ball."

He nodded slowly. "They will have to be tested at the door, as will you. With no family to register you, it will be difficult to get in."

She grinned. "We will get in. I just need to know where and when it is being held."

"Didn't my mother tell you?"

Trin shook her head. "No, she just said it was this weekend."

He exhaled, let her go and went to his desk, scribbling madly. "You have already missed the meeting of the maidens, so your next event will be the cocktail hour tomorrow afternoon and then the ball itself on Saturday."

"Cocktail hour?"

He sighed. "I will have my mother brief you. As your trainer, she has really dropped the ball."

She looked at him with amusement. "You are in charge of my education, Archivist. She wasn't the only one with a slack grip."

He sighed. "I did want to keep you hidden, but if you are in the capitol, your attendance is mandatory. Others are coming in late as well."

"Can Rish come to Creata's tomorrow? Can you ask her?" Trin looked at the paper he handed to her, folded it up, and tucked it against her collarbone for security.

"I can, but a call from you or Creata in the morning might be an excellent reminder."

She grinned. "To you or your mother?"

"A call from you in the morning? I might never get out of bed. Call my mother. She has been broody and irritated since you flew off. Hunting down your would-be assassins hasn't occupied her nearly enough."

"Is the capitol clear?"

"No. The price is now on your head from two sources, but one wants you dead, and the other wants you alive."

Trin smiled and leaned up to give him a small kiss on the cheek. "It is nice to be wanted. I will see you when it is socially appropriate to do so."

She stepped back to the edge of his window, backed out, and went invisible before she flared her wings and let the wind take her.

Trin needed a few hours' sleep if she was going to deal with the woman who would be her mother-in-law. Rish was a powerhouse in a small body that could kill with the flick of her fingers.

It was an excellent thing that Rish could be bribed with tea and cakes.

Chapter Four

Quiet laughter was not horrible to wake up to. Trin pushed herself out of bed and stumbled to the bathroom for a quick shower.

By the time she was clean and had fluffed her hair out, a set of clothes had been laid out on her bed, and the bed itself had been made. Creata's staff was efficient.

Trin pulled on the layers of clothing that she wore on a daily basis. The feel of the fabric was unmistakable, it was one of the shifting outfits that Mirbella had crafted for her. It was nice that the maid had paid attention.

When her boots were on, she checked her hair and ran a brush through it before pinning it up against the back of her skull in a semi-neat bun.

She headed downstairs, and the maid nodded toward the rear of the house. Trin walked out, and the other three were already out, sitting and having coffee and tea.

Creata smiled. "Lady Lefarge is on her way. Apparently, her son gave her a message at dawn."

"Ah, yes. I did manage to find him."

Meadra stared. "You went to visit a man, after nightfall, without an escort?"

"I flew. No one was needed." She walked over to the teapot and lifted the lid for a sniff. She grinned and poured herself a cup of *Bright Blueberry*.

She sat and nodded as she sipped before she said, "It is a good thing that she is coming. She will be far better at helping Meadra than I would."

Meadra got nervous. "Help me what?"

"Your dragon. We are going to wake her so that the valley won't have a hold on you. You will be able to choose a male of your own, and from there, you will be protected."

Meadra cupped her hands around her coffee mug. "You don't seem to need protecting."

"That is because she has been on her own most of her life." Rish's voice was calm but firm. "Trin is an excellent role model for self-sufficiency, but she still has chosen to take a mate."

Trin shrugged. "My dragon chose for

me, and Brommin hasn't objected yet."

Rish came toward them, and Creata went to stand up, but she was gracefully acknowledged and urged to remain seated.

"Brommin's dragon would chew its way out of his skull to have you as a mate. Don't doubt it. My son is just a master of self-control, or you would have been applying for authorized dispensation for an existing relationship."

Trin got to her feet and hugged her soon-to-be mother-in-law. "You are looking well, Rish."

"You as well. I hear that you have mastered invisibility."

"As much as I can." Trin smiled. "I would like to introduce you to my aunt, Meadra, and my friend, Apraxa."

Rish acknowledged Apraxa first. "I

have heard of you this week. You are Erhadenia's granddaughter."

"I am. Her daughter's bastard." Apraxa inclined her blue and crimson head.

"But still beloved, if her incessant conversations about you are any indication. Now that you have come out to the dragon court, you are welcome to join the ball."

Apraxa grinned. "I know. I checked. My gown is on the way today."

Rish inclined her head, and then, she looked at Meadra. "And you are Trin's aunt."

"Yes, Lady."

"Call me Rish. So, it is entirely likely that you have a dragon within. May I look?"

Meadra got to her feet and nodded.

"Will it hurt?"

"It won't. Let's step this way."

Trin watched as Rish walked Meadra deep into the yard, and when she had gauged the distance as appropriate, Rish took Meadra's hands and looked at her face.

Trin felt the power building, and she was glad that Meadra was wearing a shifting outfit.

Colour began to flow through Meadra's body, settling slowly on a rich purple and hot pink. Once her face and hair had set the colour, she began to expand in a slow movement that was lovely to behold.

"Oh, my." Trin watched as her aunt expanded into a dragon that was brilliant violet and hot pink. The wings were folded tightly against her back, and when the transformation was complete, she extended them, and everyone got a shock.

Meadra's wings were not a leathery construction, they were gossamer, pink, gold, and rich purple at the tips. The wings belonged on a large butterfly, not a slender dragoness.

Trin walked toward Meadra, and Rish gave her an amused and knowing look. "Your family can't do anything the regular way, can you?"

Trin shook her head. "Apparently not. Meadra, you look lovely."

The dragon looked at her and blinked huge golden eyes with long dark lashes. She was just so pretty.

Trin shifted slowly and nuzzled her aunt's cheek. The other dragon was only a third of Trin's size, but the power in her was nearly bursting out of her.

Trin nuzzled her again, and then, she slowly shifted to human. Meadra did the same.

"Did I do it? I did it, didn't I? What do I look like?"

Trin curled her lips inward for a moment. The brilliant violet with hot pink streaks was a look that her aunt would have to get used to. "You are a fairy dragon."

Rish nodded, and her expression was definitely amused. "You certainly are. They are normally seen near the mountain ranges, but you definitely are a fairy by type."

Trin put a hand on her shoulder. "And I am no longer the most obvious hair colour in the family."

Meadra immediately grabbed a

chunk of her hair and pulled it around. "Purple?"

"And pink. You have some hot pink running through your hair. It is quite lovely."

Rish laughed and laughed, doubling over.

Creata picked up her baby and came over. "What is so funny?"

Rish straightened, wiping her eyes. "The three strongest dragonesses of our generation and no one knows they will be at the ball. The city elite is going to be shocked."

Trin grinned. "I can work with shocked."

Meadra blinked. "So, I can go to the ball and pick a man?"

Trin corrected her. "Technically a mate. You and your dragon have to agree, or she will take you along for the ride. Do you hear her now?"

Meadra closed her eyes, and then, she opened them in shock. "There's a voice in my head!"

"She has always been there, but it took Rish to show her what needed to be done."

The whites of Meadra's eyes were showing. Trin took her arm. "Okay, we are going to sit down and have a cup of tea."

Creata nodded. "And breakfast. We are having breakfast."

Meadra nodded and allowed herself to be led to the table where she resumed her seat.

Creata frowned and then thrust Esty toward Meadra. "Here. Hold the baby."

Meadra took the infant out of reflex,

and she visibly relaxed when Esty was settled.

Trin returned to her seat and looked at Creata with gratitude. Creata smiled and picked up her teacup.

Their little gathering was quiet while Rish went inside to make a call.

Creata smiled. "Mirbella is also on the way, and she mentioned contacting your other supplier, who may arrive with her."

Apraxa cleared her throat. "I mentioned to her that you had run low on blades, and as she knows who makes them for you, they might be arriving together."

Trin thought of Takka and Mirbella, and while the two were both artists, their mediums were dissimilar in the extreme. "I see. This is going to be a very interesting morning."

Creata nodded and got to her feet. "I had better warn the staff."

Meadra finally came out of her daze. "Why am I holding the baby?"

Apraxa grinned. "You needed it. She calmed you right down."

Trin toasted her with the teacup. "Congratulations. When I first transformed, I got stuck. You managed in and out on your own."

Meadra nodded. "You were joking about the purple hair, right?"

"I am afraid not, but look at Apraxa. You don't even notice that she has a head like a tropical fish anymore." Trin ducked the sugar lump that came flying at her head.

"At least I don't look like I was frightened by my own reflection."

Apraxa made a face.

Trin laughed, Meadra laughed, and Apraxa winked. The joke had done its job to relieve tension in their group. When the food began to be set on the outdoor sideboard, the scent was distraction enough to keep Meadra from thinking about what she had just become.

Rish returned, and she was smirking. "You are all on the list. The invitations are being drawn up and will be delivered here in the next few hours."

Apraxa raised her brows. "Invitations?"

Rish nodded. "There will also be confirmation modules that you will hand over when you arrive. A blood sample will be suspended and analyzed, granting you your order in the choosing."

Meadra looked down at the baby and then up again. "Me too?"

"You too. This is not an opportunity that we will let pass us by."

Apraxa cocked her head. "What if my mate isn't there? What if I don't choose?"

"You will be invited to spend more time with the elite of the capitol, and if you make a choice before the next dragon ball, you will be ratified in the records."

Apraxa nodded. "Good enough. I will be there."

Creata came back out and took her daughter when she began to fuss. She fed her little one with a light gauze covering over her head for decorum's sake.

Creata smiled. "I wish I could be there."

Trin frowned. "Why can't you?"

"Dragons only, Trin. You even have to sign a non-disclosure agreement when you get there. No one that isn't a dragon is allowed to know what happens."

Rish rocked her head. "You aren't allowed to see it. You can still know what goes on."

Creata grinned. "Nice. Please, spill the details."

Rish filled her coffee cup, added cream and sugar, and sat back while she began the process of explaining the details of the most powerful beings on the planet and how they engaged in strictly monitored courtship. It was an eye-opening lecture for all of the ladies sitting around the table.

Chapter Five

To Trin's relief, Creata was loving the visitors and the conversation. Her staff brought out tray after tray of food, and Trin's stomach growled at the scents.

Creata smiled. "Help yourselves. I am stuck here until the little miss finishes."

Trin winked and balanced two plates on her arm while she went through the selections. When she was done, she slid the plate in front of her friend, and Creata grinned. "Thanks. You got all my favourites."

"Sweetie, everything is your favourite. It is your buffet."

Creata took cutlery from the maid standing by, and she stabbed the scrambled eggs, wrapping them in a strip of bacon with a deft twist.

Trin dug into her meal with a smile. Vasic might have met her because she was suitable, but he fell for Creata because she had excellent appetites. No food was made in her home that she wasn't willing to eat. As long as Trin had known her, the lioness never turned down bacon, and from hints Creata had given, she enjoyed Vasic's intimate company very much. It was nice to see what a couple could do in their first year together.

Rish cleared her throat and started the briefing. "Right, well, as you know, tomorrow is the ball, but before that is the meeting."

Trin cocked her head. "Brommin mentioned a cocktail party?"

Rish rocked her hand from side to side. "Sort of."

Meadra leaned toward Trin and asked, "Do I have a dress for that?"

Trin nodded. "You do. Do not worry."

She sighed and continued to work at her fruit salad.

A maid came up to Creata and whispered in her ear. Creata smiled. "More guests have arrived. This is turning into a weirdly fun day."

Esty was lifted to her shoulder while Creata tucked her breast away. When she was set, she burped the little mistress of the house, and the noise made all the women smile.

Rish gave Trin a sly look. "Brommin made a noise like that when he was a baby. It nearly deafened me."

Trin coughed as she caught the hint. "Uh, right." She felt heat climb in her face.

Mirbella came through the house with two assistants and Takka walking in behind her. "Okay, so cocktail dresses first. We are going to do this right here for the sake of speed."

Meadra held up her hand. "I got a gown made in Breaker City."

Mirbella gave her a long look and grinned. "Keep it for another day. Today, you are all wearing my designs."

Apraxa grinned. "Excellent. I have seen your workmanship, and I look forward to it."

"Good. You will be first." Mirbella looked to her assistants, and they erected a framework from thin rods and fabric until a changing room had been set up.

Apraxa looked down. "I am not done with my meal."

Meadra was done, so Trin volunteered her. "Mirbella, my aunt is done. She's a fairy dragon."

Meadra looked a little nervous as she got to her feet.

The seamstress looked her over and nodded. "I have something for you. Love your hair, by the way."

Meadra was whisked behind the curtain, and one assistant left the back garden to get more samples from their vehicle.

Trin listened to the surprised squawk

and guessed that Meadra had just lost her clothing to the seamstress.

Rish cocked her head. "Your aunt looks a lot like you."

Trin smiled. "Yes, close enough to be my mother. Genetically, anyway."

"So, what Makros was saying was right. They are trying to build elite dragons."

Trin nodded. "That is what is going on. Fortunately, my mother's and father's lack of self-control resulted in me. Unfortunately, it cost my grandmother my life."

"How?"

"My aunt is younger than I am, and she looks exactly like my mother."

"Oh, oooh." Rish nodded. "Right. So, this might be a problem for your father."

"No. He met my mother before her dragon was drawn out. Meadra is a completely different person. She has her own hopes and dreams and is going to find her own mate. Her life will diverge from mine, and that is a good thing. She has dreamed of life out and free. This is her chance."

Mirbella backed out of the changing area with a smirk on her face. "I am amazing."

Meadra came out, and her hair was pinned up on her head as she stepped forward wearing an opalescent gown with hints of purple in it. The gown was simple, stylish, and showed no hint of the corset. It was a classic style with gossamer panels of fabric running from shoulder to wrist. She looked delicate, feminine, and magical.

Trin smiled. "Meadra, you look wonderful."

Her aunt grimaced. "I feel naked."

Mirbella snorted. "You are wearing four layers of fabric. It just feels like nothing."

"Meadra, twirl."

Trin watched as her aunt took a few steps forward, and then, she spun. The fabric whirled out in a cascade of colour and movement. When she stopped spinning, she was smiling. "Thanks for that, Trin."

"Trin, you are next."

Trin got to her feet and smiled at Meadra. "You look wonderful."

"Thank you, Trin. Your turn."

They both went into the changing area where the assistant helped Meadra into the ball gown while the second assistant returned with armloads of garment bags.

Mirbella made sure that Meadra was getting into the formal and boned gown for the ball without issue. It was a soft mauve with gold trim that made her hair even more vibrant.

Trin removed her clothing and set it down on the ground while Mirbella found the gown she was looking for.

"Aha! Come here you wily thing." The weight of the gown was apparent when Mirbella lifted it out of the bag.

"Is this for the ball?"

"No, this is just for the introduction night. The one for tomorrow night is in a bag on its own. That one is really heavy."

The gown was pooled at her feet, and Trin got herself into it, pulling the dress upward until the weight was hanging from her shoulders. The clash of the beads was a delicate chime while Trin breathed.

"What is this?"

Meadra had left the changing area, and Mirbella was the only one there.

"This is a masterpiece. I mean, I have been looking for a client who could wear it, and you wear it very well. Go and show it to your friends if you don't believe me."

Trin was about to step out when she heard a sharp whistle. She paused and grabbed Mirbella's arm, mouthing "Stay here. Keep talking."

She went invisible, shucked off her dress, and crept out of the changing area.

Men cloaked in shadow were surrounding the gathering on the patio. Their eyes were all directed toward the changing area, but one had his arm around Meadra's throat.

Takka's bag was laid out and spilled open beyond the circle, so that is where Trin headed.

The focus was on the change room while Trin carefully grabbed the knives and crept up behind the one holding Meadra. She said a silent apology to Creata for the damage that was about to happen to her garden, and then, she moved.

All the training that Rish had given her came into play as she struck with a blade to the neck the man holding Meadra.

Rish called out. "They are venomous."

The distraction of the man howling and clutching his throat got Meadra away from the gathered assassins, and Apraxa inhaled and fired water bullets through three of the attackers. Rish dispatched two of them, leaving four for Trin.

She sprouted her wings and slashed the hands from two of the men, and when Esty let out a cry, Trin turned, and her body resumed visibility.

She felt the men behind her, but it was the two sharp shots that made her blink. Creata was standing in front of her baby's pram with her plasma blaster in her hands. Esty's cry had been her mother going for her gun.

Rish looked around and scowled. "I am going to make a call."

She pulled out her phone and spoke

in sharp tones, demanding protection.

Trin sighed. "Meadra, are you okay?"

She nodded and then looked at her dress. "I got blood on it."

Mirbella emerged, her eyes wide as she looked at the carnage. "I can get the blood out. Just hold still."

A light pink fire began on the ballgown, starting at the hem and creeping upward. Every smudge, every speck, every trace of the attack had been removed.

Mirbella looked to Creata. "Would you like me to take care of the dead?"

Creata nodded. "Please. Thank you."

More of the pink fire began under the assassins, and they flared brightly before disappearing entirely.

In five minutes, the two survivors

had been tied up, and the others had bled to death and been dispatched.

Trin had tried on both gowns and was very happy that she had gotten naked for the attack. The beads would have given her away.

The heavy beat of wings above them heralded the arrival of the dragons. Rish had called for bodyguards for the remainder of the day.

Trin got back into her daywear before she exited the changing area. The last thing she wanted was to be naked in front of dragons who might be interested in her as a mate. She had her sights set on Brommin.

The assassins had been taken into custody, and the dragon shifters were interviewing the ladies. Three men, in particular, were speaking with Meadra, and to Trin's amazement, one of those men was Torm.

With Sosa having fallen for a silver dragon and gotten a quick dispensation for an immediate mating while Trin was in Breaker City, it looked like Torm's attentions were wide open for his next target. As the dragons were at the helm for this, there was no problem that Trin could see if his dragon was choosing another likely lady. Perhaps the best match of all.

Trin watched him and smiled as his fascination for her aunt was apparent. Maybe a match would be struck.

Brommin stood in front of Trin as she continued to walk with a split focus. "Trin, do you know what happened?"

"Well, I was in the change room for most of it, but I am guessing that the guys came out of the shadows. One grabbed Meadra, so I am thinking it was the idiots in the valley who sent them to get her."

"That is a good guess. So, you were in the change room the whole time?" He arched his brow.

"Um, what did everyone else say?"

"They said that they didn't see anything. Knowing you as I do, that can only mean that you were involved." He quirked his lips.

"I may have jumped out naked as a distraction. That was toward the end."

Vasic must have arrived with the dragons. He was holding Creata and the baby and looking furious and concerned.

Creata gave Trin a look from under her lashes, and then, she winked.

Trin smiled; it was so nice to see her spirit back.

Apraxa was speaking with two more dragons, and Rish was at her side. Takka had disappeared.

"Do you know how they figured out you were here?" Brommin asked the obvious question.

Trin wrinkled her nose. "There are two guesses. One is breakfast, and the other is Mirbella."

"What?"

"Breakfast. Creata's maids went out and got enough food this morning for about nine people. That isn't normal, and it is what someone who knew my relationship with her would expect."

Brommin nodded. "Plausible."

"The other one would be to watch Mirbella because if I were in town, I

would need a dress, as would Meadra. They wouldn't know about Apraxa."

"Right. So, you are going to be at the introduction tonight?"

"I am. We all have outfits for it, so Rish just has to go through the details."

"She didn't?"

"She didn't have a chance. We do know about the confirmation scans and the non-disclosure agreement. That is about it."

He leaned down and whispered in her ear. The details were dispensed quickly, and as he moved his head, he brushed his lips against hers.

She smiled. "See you tonight."

He smiled. "Yes, you will."

She watched him go over to speak to his mother. Two days and then forever, or two days plus the engagement and then forever. After tomorrow, he would be hers.

Chapter Six

It was with great amusement that she introduced Torm to Meadra.

"Torm, I see you have met my aunt. Meadra, this is Torm. He has excellent protective and possessive instincts."

Trin blinked as Torm caught on before her aunt did.

He extended his hand, and when Meadra took it, he brought her fingers to his lips. "It is a pleasure to make your acquaintance."

Meadra blushed a brilliant red. "I feel the pleasure... I mean it is wonderful... I mean... I am glad to meet you."

Torm smiled, and he inclined his head. "I look forward to seeing you this evening."

"Me too. I mean, yes. I mean, how did you know?"

He grinned. "You just told me."

Trin backed away, and the other two dragon shifters were bemused by what was going on in front of them.

She sighed in relief. This was right. This was why Torm was attracted to her, she was the closest thing to the right woman. Well, she had been. Now Meadra was his focus.

She walked toward Apraxa, and the water dragon was only too happy to cling to Trin's arm and get away from the dragon who was interviewing her.

The man looked at Apraxa with an intense gaze, so Trin led her to one of the rosebushes. "Was he making moves on you?"

Apraxa made a face. "Yes. This group was all confirmed as selected elite mate candidates. There are eighty of them. With us, there will be eighteen ladies looking. It is one of the largest balls they have had in the last ninety years."

"Wow. Okay. That is news to me. Well, I have the details for this evening from Brommin. Once Torm leaves, I will fill you in."

"Is that the same Torm that was stalking you?"

"Yup. His dragon was going through rut and was attracted to me, but Meadra is much more his type. It seems that his dragon was looking for a specific energy pattern. So, formal introductions have been made, and it seems they have hit it off. It feels right."

Apraxa sighed and looked around the yard. "So many dead so quickly."

"Yes, and that thing you did with spitting water blades was extremely impressive."

Her friend shrugged. "It was a skill I mastered as a teen. Underwater you can't even see it. It makes fishing very quick."

"What do you think your brothers will think about this?"

Apraxa smiled. "My family will be delighted. They have wanted me to find someone for years."

"So, tonight and tomorrow you are coming along for us?"

"You will need someone to watch your back."

Trin grinned. "Thank you."

"No problem. Aside from the mayhem and the attack, I have been having a good time out here. It has certainly distracted me." Apraxa winked. "You did a very good job in keeping my work up to date."

"I needed something to take my mind off home. The shops now have enough supply to keep them in pottery, teas, and coffee for six months."

She caught a glimpse of new arrivals, and she turned in welcome.

Brenner and Niida came in, and Brenner looked at the chaos of the situation. "Trin, what the hell did you do?"

Trin grinned and walked over to hug her friends. "Nothing you wouldn't have done in my place. But, they did start it."

Niida laughed and hugged her. "And

you finished it."

"Nope, Apraxa finished it. You should see her spit."

Brenner looked surprised, but Niida giggled until she realized that Trin was serious.

Brenner looked past her and asked, "What are all the Track and Restrict agents doing here?"

Creata answered from her position against her husband, "I called them. Well, me and Rish. She called her son, I called Vasic, and here they are. They were in an etiquette briefing for this evening."

Rish clapped her hands. "Ladies, we need to finish our own briefings. Gentlemen, please take the assassins away and get as many details from them as you can. Dr. Dredock can help."

Trin looked to Brommin and inclined her head.

He grinned, grabbed one of the men, and flared his wings. He was up and out of the yard in an impressive display of thigh strength.

Apraxa whistled softly. "So, that one is yours?"

"He is. If any other female even tries, she will be up for a fight." Trin sighed. "I don't know about your dragon, but mine is exceptionally possessive."

"He does seem to have that tendency. That is why I am here, and he is there. When I am ready to face him again, I will head back to the sea."

"Well, I wish you luck with him. Did he really want control of your businesses?"

Apraxa waved her hand. "Control,

input, they are my businesses, and he has no business in them."

Trin grinned. "I can understand that."

They began to walk over to where the others were gathering. "Does he fly?"

"Yes, he does. He's a tempest." Apraxa stated it like Trin should know what that was.

"I am not from the dragon world, remember?"

"Oh, right. He's a water and air elemental but mostly air."

Trin took that to mean that he was a blowhard. She paused, turned, and walked over to Meadra and Torm.

"Torm, don't you think you should be rejoining your group?"

His eyes were glazed over with fascination, as were Meadra's. Trin wouldn't be surprised if their dragons were chatting.

"Meadra, we need to finish our briefing. We need to know what to do."

Meadra smiled sleepily. "I know what to do. I say yes to Torm, and then, we have a fast courtship."

Torm smiled. "As fast as my family will allow."

"As the only member of her family here, if I am sure you two are going to be together, I will throw whatever clout I can manage behind a speedy connection."

Torm smiled. "You were not for me."

"No, I wasn't, but now, I understand why you might have been confused about it."

He nodded, bowed a formal farewell to Meadra, sprouted his wings, and he took off with only a little hesitation.

Trin gathered Meadra with an arm around her back, and she gave her a squeeze. "Feels odd, doesn't it."

"It does. It is like something else has made up its mind and is hell-bent against anyone interfering. And she is willing to use me as a battering ram to get what she wants."

"She will. Do not doubt it for a moment. I don't know where they come from, but they are only playing in to our human sensibilities for so long. If we keep them from what they want, they will push us aside. We have given them a door into this world, and they will take it."

Meadra looked ill. "Will she hurt me?"

"No. No. Not for a minute. She wants

a mate, and you are her pathway to it. His wants a mate, and he will ride Torm to your doorstep."

"Him?"

"Torm's dragon. He is as much a part of this as yours is."

Meadra sighed as they approached the others. "This is complicated."

"Shifters have four beings in every mating. They all have to agree, or nothing can go forward, but if they are thwarted, the mating is sterile. That is what happened with my father and mother. His dragon didn't want the lady that it was engaged to, so no children."

Meadra nodded and then looked uncomfortable. "Will he want me?"

"No. His dragon was bound to my mother. When she died, so did his chance at a future."

Meadra looked at Trin. "Maybe he got exactly what he was trying for. The child of a sleeping dragoness is now one of the dragons of myth and legend."

Vasic looked away from his family. "What?"

Creata patted his chest with one hand. "Trin isn't a crystal dragon, she's a diamond."

He stared at Trin, looked down at his wife, and then back to Trin. "Is she joking?"

Trin looked around and wrinkled her nose. "No, she is not joking."

Around her were her friends and what she considered her family. Not one of the ones who didn't already know looked surprised.

Vasic looked around and sighed. "You all knew?"

Mirbella smiled. "I did, but I am a little odd."

Brenner and Niida stood together, grinning. Niida said, "When she found out she was a dragon, what else would she be?"

Vasic sighed and cuddled his family close. "Of course, she is."

Creata patted him again. "You knew she came along when you met me."

He let out a low chuffing sound that Trin had never heard from him before. It was surprisingly intimate.

"I knew, but this is going to another level. You know what this means."

"I do. We all do, but Trin isn't like that. She doesn't have any interest in ruling the world or even the city. She just wants to have her business with Brenner and spoil our children rotten.

We are enough for her."

He exhaled slowly. "Right. I need some coffee, and then, I have to get back to the Wheel. We have dignitaries coming in, and I need to be there. I will order an honour guard for our three participants in the upcoming events."

Creata smiled. "Thank you, dearest. I would be helpless without you."

He leaned down and kissed her softly. "I can smell the ozone, Creata. You are never helpless."

She was blushing and rocking little Esty when he left her for the buffet. Coffee was on his agenda but so was bacon.

The crowd of women and Brenner moved away slightly. Mirbella was firmly in their midst, and Rish was bemused by the gathering.

Brenner grinned. "This reminds me

of the time we ran from the orphanage to go camping."

Trin chuckled. "How?"

"We all bundled together with the others near the wall, and while they remained huddled, we slipped out. Who is slipping out this time?"

Creata stated. "No one. We are all staying here, and tonight, the ladies go to the cocktail party."

Rish nodded. "Right. Now, you are going to be dressed and ready by six-thirty. A car will pick you up, and you will have your invitation and the verifier. Once that is registered, you will be entered into the selection process for the ball tomorrow."

She looked at the three ladies in question and smiled, "Tonight, you will each be escorted to a kiosk where you will meet the candidates, four at a time."

Meadra cleared her throat. "The candidates?"

"The men. The men will speak with you, and you will try to determine which one you are most interested in and which come second and third if the male you choose has already been chosen by a dragoness of higher rank."

Meadra gasped. "That can happen?"

Rish nodded. "It has happened before that two females choose the same male. The females need to either choose their second pick or battle it out. For the sake of decorum, we generally urge that they try to commit to their second selection."

Trin cocked her head. "And if you know which males we are already leaning toward, you put them last in the greeting process."

Rish nodded. "It is best that way."

Apraxa smiled slightly. "And the next day, we proffer our invitations, and we are escorted into the ballroom?"

"Yes. Mingling is done until all the females are there, and then, the men form a line and the first female to choose is announced. She makes her selection and offers her hand, and when he takes it, they leave, and the next female is called up. The courtship can now begin, and Trin, if you try and stop my son from the wedding he deserves, I will make your life a living hell."

The gathering laughed at the way Rish described it as if Trin and Brommin were a sure thing. There could be a dragon out there with a higher rank by virtue of birth. There was no guarantee of the happily ever after.

Chapter Seven

With blood sample units in hand and the driver of the luxury karros smiling at them, the ladies left the vehicle and walked toward the heavily guarded archway.

Trin kept her head high as she slid over the smaller invitation and presented the verifier with her name embossed in it.

He set the small box into a much larger one and smiled. "Thank you, welcome to the night of meeting, Miss Adolla Venatrin Lem. A guide will take you to your station."

She inclined her head. "Thank you."

A young male in the livery of the dragon council was waiting for her, and he bowed low. "Miss Lem, please come with me."

She followed him and noted the few other females who were standing near tables containing snacks and beverages. So, it could be a heavy drinking evening if she was so inclined. Nice to know.

Apraxa and Meadra showed up and were stationed three tables to the left and two tables across respectively. The other stations were filled with women who looked nervous and excited. Some even looked bored.

Trin gave a little wave to her friends, and they smiled and waved back.

To her consternation, a chime rang, and panels of shadow rose from the floor, cutting off her view. Shouts of consternation were coming from the other tables.

"Ladies, please do not be alarmed. As there are more entrants than normal, we had to use an open room. An illusionist has been asked to participate in maintaining the sense of privacy. We will now begin."

It was the warning before four men walked through the barrier, and she was blinking at strangers.

She put on her best polite smile, honed behind the counter at her coffee shop, and she greeted the men, gaining their names one by one.

They were with her for ten minutes before the next batch was brought in. They greeted her, and she greeted them.

The men spoke about themselves,

and she listened encouragingly. When they left, she spoke to the third round, and so it went. Not one man asked her about herself.

The eleventh group held a surprise. Four men who were obviously water dragons walked into her space.

Introductions didn't even begin. One of them stood straight with his nostrils flaring. "You. You are the one she has been speaking to."

Trin grinned. "Yes, that would be right."

Black hair with silver and gold streaks flowed to his waist in a loose wave. His skin had the bluish sheen that the water folk often had, and his expression was pure irritation.

"Why don't you save yourself and tell her to come with me?"

Trin stepped toward him. "Do you threaten me?"

He nodded, and his men closed around her. "I do."

She stood and flared her wings out, using the tip of the right one to draw a drop of blood from his neck. "Right back at you."

His eyes widened, and he backed up, but her wingtip followed. "You are not a quartz dragon like the others have been saying."

She released her wingtip and dismissed her wings. "I am not. But... guessing is fun. Keep guessing. As for Apraxa, she is a woman who has grown up loved and supported. She has built an empire that could grow across the world. That is her passion, her creation. Don't get in the way of that and you will get along fine. Find ways to help her, and she will make you her true partner in every way."

He blinked with multiple lids. "I don't understand."

"She is under the impression that you want her businesses."

He frowned. "That was her mother's suggestion, not mine. I will take her any way I can get her."

Trin smiled and walked over, placing her hand on his wrist. "Tell her that when you are in front of her, no matter who is with you, just be forthright and leave the ego behind."

He slowly smiled. "You would be an ally?"

"I am her friend, but if you are what is best for her, you have my support. However, cross her or make her cry and

I will use my wingtip to carve you into sushi."

The men with him were standing back, respectfully, but one of them grinned.

Trin smiled. "You are the brother, I am guessing?"

His long dark hair slid forward as he bowed. "I am. Well spotted."

"Good. Stay serious, and if you could turn your backs while Apraxa and your brother speak, it would be for the best."

He bowed. "As you wish, my lady."

She nodded. "So, now we wait."

She waved at the table. "Help yourself to the food and drink."

The two men who were with Apraxa's male smiled and walked right past her toward the food.

Trin smiled and looked toward the

storm dragon. "So, what is your name? I will need to be able to recognize it when Apraxa cusses you out."

"Romak Drmor Aleghehar Wixenor." He smiled.

"Trin Lem."

He took her hand and bent his head over her knuckles. "It has been a pleasure to meet you, Trin Lem. Thank you for your advice on Apraxa."

"No problem. Your other option is to just kiss her, but she might bite."

His smile was conspiratorial. "I will consider that Plan B."

They remained in companionable silence for the remainder of the time, and he and his men left her at the chime.

Trin was getting restless. She didn't like to be boxed in, and this was definitely getting on her nerves.

She paced, and her next batch of suitors arrived. They introduced themselves, one after the other, and she nodded, but she was beginning to suffocate with all these dragons around her.

When one of the men spoke, asking her a question she hadn't heard before, she smiled.

"Did you just ask me what I was looking for in a mate?"

The man nodded. He was golden, his scent was from an area surrounded by sun-baked clay. "It seems to me that if I don't find a mate here, I might want to take into consideration what a woman might want in a mate."

She searched her memory and smiled. "It is a good question, Nolesander Kreelo. I would say, that what a mate wants, what anyone wants, is to have their mate be the best that they can be, and in turn, she will do her best. Together, they lift each other up, and they are both much stronger than either could ever be apart."

The other men had begun to stare at her, and some of the arrogant façades that had developed over the waves of fawning women in the other cubicles faded at her blunt words.

"Dragons control this part of the world because we are wise and even-tempered. That said, I have met a lot of jackasses since my dragon woke, and many others are known and reported on around the world. Dragons have tre-mendous power, but it doesn't make us innately better than humans or other shifters. It merely means that we have more to control and that control is what can lead to arrogance. It also means that when a dragon goes wrong, it can de-·stroy their family, friends, and all around them. Keep that in a part of your mind with every heartbeat, every step, and every word you speak to those around you carries the weight of what you are. When I thought I was human, when they marked me as human, I had a human's freedom to speak whatever came into my head. I knew that those words could hurt, so I tempered them. I did that with no power, no innate right to obedience. I could still make folk quail before me, just with words. My first meeting with a dragon was with a frustrated female whose insecurity caused her to lash out. I was able to answer back, but it cost me my humanity and all that it meant to me."

The dragons behind Kreelo were staring with wide eyes.

"So, just be the man that you would want your mother to have had in her life or your sisters or your nieces, aunts, and friends. Act in a way that makes them proud to stand next to you, knowing that you have done all you can to be worthy."

A silver dragon asked, "What about the women? What do they do for us?"

"We are the ground under your feet. The house that you take shelter in. If you undermine a woman, she will become the sliding sands of the wind-swept desert. She is made of the same stone but has been shattered so many times that she can no longer reliably support you if you need it. Keep her safe, keep her whole, and you will live a long and happy life."

The young man asked, "What if we don't get along?"

"That is easy. Let your dragons talk. Go somewhere, you shift and she shifts, and your dragons will compete for dominance or come into a treatise. When you return to human, you will understand what is going on and how you should proceed. We are not alone in this, our dragons make this choice, and we learn to live with it."

Kreelo smiled. "It isn't romantic."

She thought about the first time that her dragon had identified Brommin as *the pretty one*. "It has its moments."

"That is why the courtship is so important. Once our dragons make up their minds, the human parts of us have to make up for the suddenness of the decision." Kreelo smiled.

She reached out and took his hand. There was a shop, the scent of herbs, and a woman with brown and gold hair. The scent of magic was in the air around her, and it was tinged with the scent of fascination. "Oh, so you..."

"This is for my father. My dragon has already chosen."

Trin smiled, suddenly at ease with what was going on. "I wish you luck, Nolesander. Keep in touch after you find your lady's heart. I suspect that she is holding many secrets."

"Her father hates the dragons, so yes, I am guessing that I have a battle ahead of me." He smiled and the corners of his eyes crinkled. He was looking forward to the fight.

The chime rang, and her amused

gathering left.

Torm was in the next group, and he looked nervous and determined. "Lady Lem, I am glad to see you."

She grinned. "Have you seen Meadra yet?"

He shook his head, and the other men with him looked confused.

She chuckled and took his hand. "It will be fine. You are her dragon's choice. No one else is even visible to her eyes. It explains your fixation. You were close to what you wanted, but I was not it."

The other males were all of a higher draconic ranking, but aside from greeting them politely, she had no interest when they reeled off their accomplishments.

She was waiting for the next group, and Torm smiled. "It is horrible in its way. The waiting." He squeezed her hand, and she realized that she was still holding it.

"You do realize that after the final choosing and the binding, you are going to be my uncle or my stepfather, depending on which version you want to embrace."

His eyes widened, and he laughed. "I look forward to it, niece."

The chime rang again, and he and the others left.

She paced back and forth again as she waited. They had to be near the end. Brommin had to be close.

When the last group came through, there were only three of them.

She cocked her head. "Are you the last?"

They nodded, confused. "We are.

This is the last round. We have seen the other females."

That was it. It was the final straw to an evening of frustrations. She spread her wings and left her cubicle, searching for her mate.

Chapter Eight

Her dragon offered up extra senses so that she could follow Brommin.

The glow of his aura was up and on the fourth floor, so she smashed through one of the twenty-foot windows of the ballroom and headed outside.

The sight of him through a window, bloody and chained, filled her with fury. She dove for the window, wrapping her wings around her at the moment of impact.

She stood in the space in front of Brommin and glared at the ten younger males who were carrying weapons.

"Why?"

One of the bolder males in his early twenties snarled. "He won't even consider one of our sisters. You are a filthy human-born dragon. Abomination, you shouldn't even exist."

She cocked her head and smiled grimly at them. She lashed out with her wings and cut the chains from Brommin. He got to his feet, and he murmured, "Don't kill them."

She nodded, and her dragon took over.

When she held up her hands and spouted diamond claws, three tried to run for the exit. A swish of her wings and the door closed.

She grabbed and grappled with each of the men, some attacked her wings and learned how sharp they were, her claws cut faces, one by one until each of the ten who had hauled off her beloved were marked and stained by their complicity in the evening's work.

Brommin began knocking heads together, and eventually, they were the only two standing. He came to her and wrapped his arms around her. "I am sorry that this happened. I expected them to attack you, not me."

She sighed and pressed her head to his chest. "I still choose you."

"Good. We might have a few minutes left. Hold tight and pull in your wings."

She let him cradle her in his arms, and he spread his wings, walking to the window she had shattered and launching them into the night and back the way she had come.

He cruised through the window of

the ballroom and directly toward her cubicle. His landing was a little rough, but he was there in time. She held him tight, and the other men didn't ask what had happened.

When the chime sounded, she was still in his arms. The walls of darkness dissipated, and those gathered were exposed.

Brommin walked to the couch in the corner, retracted his wings, and he settled down.

She looked at him and winced. His cheek was swollen, his eye was red, there was a cut on his lip that went from top to bottom. "They hurt you."

He smiled. "I will be fine by dawn. Thank you for coming for me."

"I don't know how important it was for you to be here, but I knew you would never avoid a chance to have me in your arms."

"Never. If they hadn't gotten me by surprise, I would have found my way to you in every grouping."

"And thereby driving the organizers insane."

He sighed. "Just as we are doing now. You are meant to be talking with others."

She sighed and pressed a quick kiss to his lip, exhaling gently, and her dragon added a certain something. She pulled his head toward her and kissed the swollen side of his eye, pressing light and tiny kisses along his cheekbone. She sat back and watched as the marks of his injuries faded and healed before her eyes.

She was quite pleased with herself.

He smiled. "I am not surprised. You are going to be the most powerful dragon of our generation. What do you plan to do with it?"

She smiled. "Open that extra shop, and then, we will see what comes."

"Nothing more?"

"Maybe work on that archive, making copies. There are things in there that the female dragons need to know, and if I can get that across with a pamphlet campaign, I will do it."

He squeezed her, and other heads around the room were staring at them.

Trin glanced around and sighed. "It looks like we are going to have a lot of uphill work ahead."

Meadra stepped toward them, blocking some of the faces. Torm formed an additional brick in the fence. Soon, several of the folk she had spoken to that evening, including Apraxa and her would-be mate. They shielded them effectively from the gazes of those in the room.

"It will be different tomorrow night. Tomorrow, your dragon will be announced when your name is spoken. They will at least be more respectful to your face after that." He whispered it in her ear.

"I don't want respect, I just want to be left to my own devices. My dragon demands her mate, and you are..."

He sighed. "It is hard to define, isn't it?"

"Yes. Very."

"As long as you choose me tomorrow night, I can help you."

She grinned. "There is literally no one

else on my mind."

They sat for a moment more. Brommin smiled. "Nice dress, by the way."

"Thank you. You are looking smudged but very official tonight as well. How are the parts that they bound with chains? Why didn't you just sprout wings and snap out of them?"

"It does not work that way for me. Not all of us are made of diamond."

Apraxa's mate whipped around, and he stared for a moment before she elbowed him in the ribs, and he turned back around.

"Since we have privacy..." Trin looked at Brommin and pulled his head down for a kiss.

They continued to kiss until Brommin paused. When Trin's hearing came back to her instead of the roar of passion in her ears, she heard nothing.

"Is your mother standing right behind me?"

Brommin's lips quirked. "My father. So, not as bad as it could be."

"My son, why are you manhandling one of the choosers?"

"Lord Lefarge, how nice to hear your dulcet tones." Trin pivoted on Bromnin's lap as carefully as she could manage considering their proximity.

"I have found a number of novice guards in one of the upper rooms. They were all marked with three claw marks on the cheek. There were also chains and a scattering of those beads that you are wearing."

Brommin kept his arms wrapped around her. "Do you think it has anything to do with her?"

The senator came over and murmured quietly. "It has everything to do with her. The scent of both of you was all over those men. Did they kidnap her?"

Brommin helped Trin to her feet, and he stood behind her. "No. They took me, Father. They wanted to keep me from making this essential meeting. Without Trin's pre-approval, I would not be able to appear at tomorrow's ball. I was shackled above, so she came and got me."

"Right. Well, that is a different matter. Thank you, Lady Lem, for going in search of my son. I will deal with those who attacked him. Of course, you made them easy to spot."

Trin smiled brightly. "My dragon tells me that those wounds won't heal.

She can grant them healing, but the scars will remain."

"I am still not sure that you are, what everyone thinks you are, but the evidence is adding up."

Trin looked at the small army of those willing to defend her privacy, and she sighed. "Yes, it really is."

The vehicle that took them home was the senator's private karros.

Meadra still had a dazed smile on her lips. Her first kiss with Torm had been rushed, but it had been intense.

Apraxa was a little bemused. Whatever her would-be-lover had said was sinking in.

Trin was both exhausted and exhilarated. The young men she had wounded would be dealt with after tomorrow's ball.

They were delivered back to Creata and Vasic's home without anything eventful happening.

Creata's first words reminded her that the evening had been fairly eventful. "Trin, do you realize that your gown is spattered with blood?"

Trin looked down and winced. "Mirbella is going to kill me."

The once white and iridescent gown was now the victim of snapped columns of beads and spattered with blood.

"She will have to wait until tomorrow. For tonight, I have a meal prepared. You can all get out of your gowns and into sleepwear, and then, we will discuss as much as you are able to."

Trin nodded and didn't hug her friend. No one needed to be smeared with blood after ten in the evening.

"I get the hint. Pyjama party it is." She headed upstairs, leading the other two.

A light scrubbing and a nail brush later, she was free of blood, dressed in a nighty and robe that Creata provided for her guests, and sitting down with the other ladies drinking herbal tea and eating small sandwiches.

Creata asked the question. "Well, how was it?"

Meadra cleared her throat. "Better than expected but stranger, too. There were dragons from all regions and some from overseas."

Trin gave her a wry look, and Meadra smiled. "I am not giving away any secrets. Just vague descriptions."

Creata leaned forward. "I am married with a baby, I crave as much vagueness as I can get."

Apraxa sat back and smiled. "You are seated in a small space, and suddenly, four male dragons walk through the wall and introduce themselves. They stand there and talk at you, not to you, and then, a chime rings and they move on to the next female."

Trin chuckled. "And then, there is that exciting moment when a stranger from a strange land tries to attack you, and you have to defend yourself."

Meadra smiled. "Or the curtains come down, and you are in the lap of your chosen male."

Trin blinked and then realized that no one had seen her. None of the females or males had seen her take off, they had only seen her in Brommin's lap, spattered with blood.

"You guys didn't see that, and you came to help me anyway? Aw, how sweet." Trin smiled. "I had to go and rescue Brommin from a set of young guardsmen who were upset that he had made himself available to me instead of one of their female relatives."

Apraxa sat up. "What?"

"Oh, yeah. They had him chained up. I set him free and then gave the young men something to remind them that messing with the mating process is not allowed."

"And then?" Creata took a huge bite out of her tiny sandwich, endangering her fingers.

"He flew us back to my cubicle just in time for the shadows to drop." Trin snagged some more food and sat back to eat. She mumbled, "There may have been some kisses exchanged, but then, the senator showed up and our relaxing moment was over. I honestly thought they would come after me."

Meadra and Apraxa asked her question after question, but she smiled and shook her head. "No one knows what I am yet. It is just us, our friends, and Brommin's family. Tomorrow will be the public reveal. I am just hoping that no other dragon female outranks me."

Meadra stared at her, and then, she started laughing. "That is very funny. That is the funniest thing I have heard all evening."

Trin smiled and sipped at her tea. "How was your introduction with Torm in the room?"

She smiled shyly. "He kept all the men in a corner, facing the wall while he stroked my hand and my cheek."

Apraxa smiled and turned her head to Trin. "Did you know that Romak was here for this?"

Trin shrugged. "I had a feeling. I didn't call him if that was your worry. I am guessing that he checked and you weren't home, so he thought of the next largest gathering of dragons and came here. He was probably panicking a little."

"He's arrogant, so panic isn't his forte. He simply expects things to go his way."

Trin asked, "Did you talk?"

Apraxa nodded. "We did. I think he is salvageable."

It was high praise from the hurricane

dragon.

Creata was nibbling on food with her eyes wide. "Will you talk about this sort of thing after the ball?"

Trin winked. "We have a non-disclosure agreement. Of course, we will."

Chapter Nine

Four hours of sleep was all that Trin was going to get. She slipped on her robe and walked down the stairs and to the rear of the house.

The nearly full moon was setting, and it made her smile. Of course, the ball would be held at the full moon. It made no sense because the dragons wouldn't be affected by it, but it would make it harder for the females to fly off when they had to make their choice.

Trin stood out where the wind could pull at her robe, and she breathed in and out.

She sensed Vasic before she heard his footfalls. "Are you nervous, Trin?"

She inclined her head slightly. "My human mind is in a whirling panic, and my dragon is digging her claws in. She wants him, and I don't really have a say in this anymore."

He walked close to her and stood a few feet away, looking at the same moon she was. "It was the same for me. I looked at Creata and saw a sweet and timid creature. I didn't want sweet and timid, I wanted fire. My lion knew what he wanted, and he saw the mother of his children the moment that he looked at her."

She chuckled. "When did you find out?"

"After the engagement had been announced. We were scheduled for a chaperoned trip to the ballet, and I arrived early at her grandmother's home. I heard the clash of loud music and off-key singing. I followed the caterwauling, and there she was, working with a ratchet to assemble some sort of wiring harness."

"Her singing has always been an acquired taste." Trin smiled softly.

"Esty loves it. But, she looked at me, and I actually saw her, dressed in her evening gown without a smudge on her and surrounded by metal, cables, and computing devices. I finally saw *her*."

"And you knew."

"I knew. Much to her surprise, I kissed her, and we completed our courtship and booked the wedding that week. I finally learned to trust my lion. He had seen what I wasn't even looking for. My mate." Vasic's voice was soft.

"Regrets?"

"I wish I had seen the signs that she was being smothered by the niceties of family, obligation, and motherhood."

"She was gotten to in time, and you now know what to do."

He chuckled. "Her lab was always waiting for her. She had to decide it was time to return to it."

Trin inhaled and exhaled slowly. "It was. Her inventions have always ridden just above public technology, and she could do amazing work if she just let herself go."

Vasic chuckled again. "Perhaps wait until the breastfeeding is over before you encourage her to lose track of the world around her."

"Perhaps you should trust your wife

to know what is best for her daughter." Creata's amused tone rippled through the night.

Vasic turned, but Trin kept her head trained skyward. The stars were fading, and the light was slowly edging along the eastern horizon.

She stood and watched the sunrise with her friend and her husband, the first mated couple in her little circle.

Unlike Vasic, she had only had knowledge of her beast for just over a month. Trusting her dragon was the sticking point for her. The dragon gave her power and protection, but what did it want in return, and what did it want from Brommin?

Trin was reading a book to Esty when Mirbella came into the room.

"There you are! I have been looking for you for ten minutes."

"Why? I fitted the gown yesterday."

"I have made some alterations. Takka has offered a few enhancements, and I installed them. You need to be walked through their release procedures."

"A moment." Trin continued reading until she finished the last six pages of the fairy tale.

The nanny that had been waiting nearby came to retrieve her charge. Trin kissed Esty on the head and then handed her over.

It was time to get dressed for the ball.

Trin went through the locations of all the fine and deadly filaments that had been secreted in her gown. She was still wearing an ancient-styled tunic, but the back-laced corset that wrapped around her waist and supported her breasts was loaded with everything from razor-thin blades to small smoke bombs.

"Why is she giving me all of this?"

"Because there is a price on your head. It is a very large price, and while Takka isn't interested, others might be."

She looked to Mirbella. "A wizard wouldn't be?"

Mirbella didn't take offense. "I am much better off with the diamond dragon as my friend than I would be if I tried to end her reign before it started."

"I am not going to reign. That has never been in my plans."

Mirbella chuckled. "The world has changed, but it hasn't seen a diamond dragon for a very long time. It will react to you, one way or another. I hope

Brommin knows what he is in for."

Uncertainty rocked through her, and she swayed. "I am not sure that he does. Oh, no."

Mirbella held her upright when she would have sat down. "Oh, no. You are not going to sit in this thing until after you have chosen your mate. The silk is lovely and flowing, but it doesn't like direct pressure."

Trin glanced toward the fading light of the sunset. "So, I am on my feet until midnight?"

"I believe that the moon's zenith will be somewhere nearer ten thirty."

"Four hours then. I can be on my feet for four hours." She watched as Mirbella fluttered the skirts and checked to make sure that the fall remained decorous.

"Do the others have boots?"

"No, they have the proper slippers. You needed something to hold the crystal spikes."

She smiled slightly. "I do feel better knowing that I can defend folks if the valley idiots show up. They are the only ones who have a claim on Meadra."

"And you."

"No. The Home for the Unknown had to name me, so they had to legally sign on as my family. At the same time, all ties to family past or present had to be severed. The notice was posted in the papers, and no one showed up to claim me. Their time in my life has passed. Even my father has no claim."

"Have you met him yet?"

"No, I think that facing him will be better done when Brommin and I have our link. I have a few things I want to say to him, and I might need a witness, so I don't hurt him."

"You are mad?"

"Furious, but she was desperate to escape, and he thought he couldn't get her pregnant. It was monumental stupidity on both parts."

Mirbella sighed and stepped back. "You are beautiful. The gown is beautiful, even the armoured corset is lovely. You are a vision, and Brommin will be stunned."

"I doubt it. I am pretty sure that he is never stunned. Are the others wearing the same thing?"

Mirbella rocked her hand a little. "More or less. The idea is to give the males a hint of your colour before you arrive. Dressing you in clear was out of the question, so I chose white and crystal. They might still think you are a crystal dragon, but we know the truth, and so does Brommin."

Trin nodded and took a deep breath. "Right. No surprises. He knows."

Footsteps rapidly approached the door, and Creata opened Trin's door. "The karros has been destroyed."

Trin nodded. "As I expected. I am going to fly us there."

Mirbella blinked. "All of you?"

"I can do it in my human form with just my wings. We will look correct when we arrive though I may crease their gowns a little."

Mirbella whistled. "Wow. Okay. You can... all right."

Creata blinked. "You are going to fly there?"

"I am. This outfit can shift with me,

so we will just get to the top of the house and fly from there."

Mirbella nodded. "It can shift with you. It took most of last night, but it will shift with you."

Trin smiled and put a hand on the designer's shoulder. "I know. I was hoping that this would all be a normal night of blushing and giggling. Now, I am ready for what happens as the backup plan."

Creata sighed and smiled. "You look amazing. I wish I looked half that good on my wedding day."

"You did. You glowed, though part of that might have been nervousness."

Creata chuckled. "I still didn't look half as majestic as you do right now."

"Let's hope that the night flight doesn't ruffle my hair." Trin grinned.

Mirbella gave her one final look. "There you are. You are perfect. Not a hair out of place."

"It never lasts long, but thanks for the compliment. I was designed to be scruffy." Trin winked.

She straightened her shoulders and walked to Creata, giving her a gentle hug. "Where are the others?"

"In the drawing room."

"Good. I am going to get them to the roof, and we will go from there."

She grabbed her invitation and tucked it inside her corset. With her mind focused on action, she headed downstairs.

Trin swept into the drawing room with her gown fluttering. She paused. "You two look amazing."

Meadra was wearing a bright violet

with hot pink-embroidered trim gown, wrapped with gold cording. Her hair was a pile of curls that exposed her neck. She looked delicate and lovely.

Apraxa was a study in power. Her gown was patterned with blue waves, and thin crimson streaks ran through it turning the design into storms where the red coalesced. Her hair was twisted together into a thick column that hung over her shoulder and down to her waist.

Apraxa held her invitation up. "We would be sitting ducks out there. So, what do we do?"

"Give me your invitations and get on the roof. We are flying there."

Meadra blinked. "Torm said there would be press. They can't come inside, but they love to get images of the queens arriving.

"I will try and let us down slowly, so our skirts don't fly."

Apraxa cackled and clapped her hands. "Let's go. The sooner we are there, the sooner we will be on our way to our men."

Meadra handed over her invitation with a smile. "Take us to the ball, niece."

Apraxa followed suit. "Try not to ruffle my hair."

"That is up to the wind, friend. Try and hang on."

They all headed up to the roof via the attic rooms. Meadra and Apraxa were wearing sandals, so Trin got into place and held out her hands.

She gathered Meadra in her left arm and Apraxa in her right. Her wings bellied out, and she took a deep breath.

Creata and Vasic were watching them from the window, and Creata gave them a thumbs-up. "Don't be late. And don't flash your undercarriage."

Trin lifted her friends off their feet before they could hesitate, and she jumped off the four-story roof. Down below, she made out a few folk who were watching and who scrambled for vehicles. It was time to put some speed on without ruffling their hair.

Her dragon provided them with a wall of energy that led the wind to slip around them, and they crossed the city in under a minute.

Lights started flashing below them as they approached the grand hotel where the ball was being held. It seemed that the press was out in force.

Trin murmured on the descent, "Ladies, check your skirts. We are landing right in front of them."

With that last warning, she landed right in front of press representatives from across the new world.

The light was blinding.

Chapter Ten

Trin's eyes adapted to the light, and she took her friends by the hand, leading them past the reporters who stepped aside as she approached.

She walked them to the entryway, guarded by a bemused elder dragon with dark hair liberally streaked with silver. She produced their invitations, sorted them out, and handed hers to the man watching the door.

He smiled. "You would be the one who has chosen Brommin."

She inclined her head. "One of them, I am sure."

"The whispers about your defense of your mate last night have spread far and wide. Those who had an inkling for him have wisely chosen others."

She smiled brightly. "Good."

"Please enter, and may you find peace in your choice." He waved her through.

She nodded and entered the doors that were being held open by some younger dragons, who watched her pass with interest.

Once inside, she checked her gown for wrinkles and scowled at the stray curl that had made it down to hang against her collarbone.

Meadra came inside with a blush on her cheeks, and Apraxa was laughing brightly.

"What did I miss?" Trin grinned at

the contagious amusement.

"A gust of wind and Meadra's quick hands. She nearly showed her lack of underpinnings to all and sundry in front of the cameras."

Apraxa glanced back. "And there are a number of irritated ladies who got out of their karros to a sadly distracted audience."

Trin shrugged. "They shouldn't have sent their siblings to wreck the Tals' karros."

The line of honour guards was a good clue as to where they were to go.

Apraxa muttered, "You are certain it was them?"

"I am. I caught the scent on Creata when she came up to me. There were young dragons just after their first shift. Younger brothers are my best guess."

Meadra was still blushing as she walked next to Trin. "I can't believe that almost happened."

Trin chuckled. "I read up about fairy dragons. You attract airborne imps and other magic."

Meadra blinked. "But why now?"

"Because now you are a dragon, sweetie, not just a potential genetic carrier." Trin whispered it as the line of guards directed them into a huge ballroom.

There were two small clusters of ladies in the room, and when their trio entered, there were eleven total females in the space.

Trin led her group to the bar and asked for some sparkling soda.

"Yes, miss, for the others?"

"The same. This isn't the night to lose

one's head."

He smiled. "Of course."

She watched as his hands moved smoothly over the tops of the glasses, and she shook her head when she saw the telltale fizz. "On second thought, we will get our refreshments elsewhere."

He paused and paled when he looked at her expression. He whispered an apology and removed bottles from under the counter. "Here. These have not been tampered with."

She took the bottles, inhaled, and confirmed that it was just plain soda. "Thank you."

She passed the bottles to Apraxa and Meadra, who looked at them, shrugged, and as one, they put the caps on the edge of the bar and smacked the bottle.

There was a light fizz, and they gig-

gled. Trin made sure that all three were clear before they drank.

They walked to the windows, and Trin was shocked. "When did we climb stairs?"

Meadra smiled. "The twelfth member of the guard."

"The larger hotels have had enchantments put on the stairs so that they are not taxing. I am guessing that we went up three flights of stairs in that compressed space." Apraxa sipped from the bottle and looked over at the giggling groups of women.

Trin chuckled. "I think we look a little low class, drinking from the bottle."

Meadra shrugged. "I am low class. I am a farm girl."

"I am a shark-raised bastard who does international trade. I have had worse things to drink in slightly more bizarre conditions."

They laughed and watched as the final seven women arrived, heads high and knowing their worth.

Trin's dragon did an assessment, and none of the other ladies were even close to the level of their little gathering. If the order of selection went by power level, Trin and her group could gather up all the men and keep them.

She was idly wondering if she would collect all the brunettes, Apraxa the blondes, and Meadra the redheads when a loud gong sounded, and a voice rang out. "Would all of the choosers please line up at the edge of the room? Your candidates are about to enter."

Trin and her group were already at the edge of the room, so they stood by, sipping their sodas.

"Ladies, thank you for attending, I would like to announce the men available for your selection." The voice was familiar.

Trin smiled when she recognized the voice of the man who took her invitation at the door.

She stopped smiling when the sound of marching rippled through the air and under her feet. Two huge doors at one end of the ballroom opened, and the male dragons marched in, in a straight line. They lined up in rows of twenty, each man three feet from the one next to him. Four rows deep they stood, and each one had Trin's attention.

She had been expecting to see them in a military uniform, not wearing wide-legged, pleated black trousers, a belt to hold them up, and nothing else.

Trin fought her dragon because it wanted to sweep through and snatch Brommin from the collection of eligible males in front of her. They were nice, but only one was her pretty one.

Trin was amused by the ladies who moved to put themselves in front of her. If it wasn't a free for all, they were going to have to wait, just like the rest of them.

The man from the door appeared, and his bronze wings were gleaming in the lights of the ballroom.

"Ladies, as this is your first choosing, and hopefully, your only one, the rules will be as follows. Yesterday, the blood samples were taken and analyzed. The most powerful dragon among you will choose first."

He stepped in front of the men, and

he smiled. "The one selected to choose will step forward, identify herself for the record, and shift enough to prove her identity. It can be a hand, a wing, or your features. Take your pick. As long as we can confirm that you are what the tests identified, you have your choice of the men remaining in formation.

"Once you have selected and made your choice, he has the right of refusal. If he refuses immediately, you may move on to your second choice."

Trin blinked. She had never considered that Brommin would refuse.

The master of ceremonies smiled and nodded. "Right. Now, if you are ready, we will begin."

Everyone held their breath; the choosing was about to start.

He looked at his tablet, and then, he

cleared his throat. "Diamond dragon. Step forward please."

The gasp that ran through the gathering included sharp inhales from the men.

Trin waited until the fuss cooled, and then, she set her bottle at the edge of the windowsill, and she turned toward the women blocking her path. She stepped forward and transformed her body, making her skin diamond hard from head to toe. The ladies who had their backs to her were simply pushed aside by her body. They cried out and stumbled but went quiet when they actually looked at her.

"I am Adolla Venatrin Lem, daughter of LeeHee Anders, daughter of Lord Minnet, designated human at birth and raised by the Home for the Unknown. I am a diamond dragon."

The master of ceremonies looked a little weepy, but he nodded. "Identification has been accepted. Make your choice."

She walked through pathways in the gathered men, and she moved straight to Brommin. She held out her hand, palm up. "Do you accept me?"

He grinned and took her hand, pulling her against him. "I accept you with a joyful heart."

She smiled and shifted from diamond to flesh as he kissed her. She kissed him with enthusiasm, and when he lifted her off her feet and walked her out of the block, she simply went along for the ride.

She whispered against his lips. "Is this it?"

He chuckled. "This is the beginning."

She held onto him and hoped that he was right.

* * * *

"The next dragon is the fairy dragon."

Meadra nearly choked. She had thought for sure that Apraxa had higher value.

Apraxa took her soda and winked. "Go and announce yourself."

The murmur in the room was less shocked, and most of the folks were still staring at Trin and Brommin in their comfortable embrace.

Meadra stepped forward, and she wasn't sure what she was supposed to do. Her dragon was amused, but it helped with a burst of power that tinted her skin a brilliant purple with stars made of magic moving under the colouration.

She stood in front of the men and looked at the master of ceremonies. "I am Meadra Anders, daughter of the Delarm Valley, aunt to the diamond dragon, and I am a fairy dragon."

The master of ceremonies blinked. "Her aunt?"

She nodded. "I am her aunt on her mother's side."

"Acknowledged and recorded. Approach your mate."

She nodded, breathed in, and walked through the columns of men until she was standing in front of Torm. Her dragon was shrieking, but Meadra followed Trin's example. She held out her hand and said softly, "Do you accept me?"

Torm placed his hand in hers and pulled her to him, kissing her hard. "I accept all that you are."

Her lips throbbed, and she let her magic drain away. They walked to the side where Brommin and Trin were waiting and stood behind them.

She kept glancing at Torm, and she couldn't believe it. It was done. She had chosen her mate. All she needed to do was make it to the wedding, and her family would never be able to touch her.

She swayed in relief, and he put his arm around her protectively. Tears pricked her eyes as she realized that the only other comfort she had ever gotten had come from Trin. This was a new life and a new start, it just remained to be seen how soon the new portions could start.

* * * *

Apraxa waited. It was possible that there was another dragon who was stronger than she was, but it wasn't likely.

"Would the hurricane dragon please step forward."

Apraxa had already set the beverages down, so she took on the body pattern of her dragon, scaly blue with scarlet hair and black eyes. It was a riveting look, and she knew it.

She moved silently, and the women that she passed jumped in shock at her appearance. It took land walkers a bit of time to get used to the look of a sea dragon.

She settled in front of the men and grinned with her deadly teeth exposed. "I am Apraxa Tiburon, daughter of Harusha, the siren of the North Sea and Morix Tiburon, shark shifter and family master. My grandparents are Menoral and Riika, king and queen of the ocean city. I am the hurricane dragon."

A breeze in the room started to move fabric, and when she got the nod, she walked through the rows, one row at a time until she got to Romak. She didn't ask him, she grabbed him by the back of his neck and pulled his mouth to hers, dismissing the bladed teeth before contact.

Their kiss was intense, and his addition to the wind in the room was wild. Her skirt flared up, and he held it down with his palm. "I will take you, Apraxa, for all that you are. I accept your proposal."

She grinned. "I have made my choice."

Apraxa let the wind diminish, and she led him to the position where the line was forming.

He leaned down and whispered to her, "Your colouration is astounding."

She blushed. Strong colours were a sign of fertility, and her colouration was unmistakable. "Thank you. I find your smoke and fire very pleasing as well."

His fingers wove with hers, and she leaned against his shoulder. They had been engaged since they were children, but with the declaration and action in front of witnesses, it was official.

Apraxa kept her head forward, but her fingers curled in tight to Romak's. It had been a bit of a fight, but they were together now.

The only thing that could mess this up was themselves.

Chapter Eleven

Trin watched as the next dragon was called. There was a sapphire dragon who had a problem proving her power. When she finally managed to make her hands blue, she was allowed to continue.

She made a beeline for her chosen mate, and he smiled and accepted her. They hugged and then joined the lineup.

The colours streamed through, the gemstones and then the metallics.

One woman, one of the three topaz dragons, was rejected by her choice.

Tears wobbled in her eyes, but she lifted her chin and moved to the back row, extending her hand to her second choice. He was very classy about it. He accepted her and drew her to him with a tender expression.

Trin let out the breath she had been holding. Her dragon reached out and took the woman's hand as they passed her. The huge golden eyes were wide and her mouth opened in surprise as she received the surge of energy.

The woman stared at her hand as she and her second choice took their position in line.

Brommin leaned down. "What did you do?"

"The dragon gave her a blessing."

His smile was smug. "I thought as much. I wonder when it will manifest?"

"After they have sex. It was a fertility blessing."

He blinked. "You can do that?"

"Apparently. I am new to this. This time last year I was worried about getting the coffee shipment on time."

They stood and watched as the metallic dragons made their choices. Two of the oceanic dragons were chosen, much to their delighted surprise.

The copper dragon was the last up. She announced herself and walked up to the man who had rejected the topaz dragon. She asked him softly if he would accept her, and she was only halfway through the question when he lunged forward and hugged her tight.

Trin leaned against Brommin's arm, and she sighed. "That was nice."

"They have been an item since they

were teenagers, but her family isn't powerful. She's a copper, he's a gold, I am glad they were able to connect. He would never be allowed to attend another ball if they didn't."

"So, once rejected, you can't return?"

He quirked his lips. "No, if you reject a female, you surrender your right to attend subsequent events."

"Wow. It is a good thing you didn't turn me down." She smiled.

He wrapped an arm around her reinforced waist, and he grinned. "Never."

The master of ceremonies looked around, and he clapped his hands. "Gentlemen, thank you for your participation. Good luck on the next day of choosing. Thank you for attending."

The dismissal was absolute. The words were lighthearted, but the tone wasn't. Those men would leave or face the elder dragon.

The single men filed out and left the room.

The elder looked at the line. "Now, young couples, the upper levels of the hotel are yours to play with. First, introduce yourselves in the dance, and then, you can seek out privacy to get acquainted with your mate."

Trin was shocked. She looked at Brommin. "Did you know about this?"

"I was aware of it, yes."

She gave him a dark look. "Hmm. This shady side of you is rather intriguing."

He laughed and then noted that the master of ceremonies was coming up to them. "I believe I should make an introduction."

Trin blinked. "Okay."

He offered her his arm, and she accepted, walking to meet the master of ceremonies halfway.

"Senator Weekon, this is my mate, Trin. Trin, this is Senator Amathor Weekon, your grandfather."

Trin blinked slowly and then one more time. "Did you say, grandfather?"

Senator Weekon smiled and extended his hand. "As you are my son's child, I am your grandfather. You are very welcome to our family."

She extended her hand to his and noted that her fingers were shaking. Aside from Meadra, he was the first person to claim her as blood.

"I am pleased to meet you, Senator Weekon. You knew who I was when I arrived?"

"I suspected. I never guessed that my son's daughter would be the diamond dragon that has been making herself known around town."

She wrinkled her nose. "That happens when you have assassins at your door. They are disruptive little buggers."

His eyes widened and then narrowed. "Tell me more."

She opened her mouth, but Brommin stopped her. "Perhaps we can come by your home or office tomorrow?"

Senator Weekon's cheeks darkened. "Yes, of course. Enjoy your evening. I will call Makros."

Brommin smiled. "Thank you."

Music had started up in one corner of the ballroom, and Brommin led her there.

"I don't really dance. I mean, Brenner and I learned with Creata, but it was a decade ago."

He smiled. "Just trust me to keep you from bumping into anyone, and we will be fine."

He swung her around, and she settled against him. Her left arm settled on his shoulder, and all that bare skin was driving her to distraction.

"So, why do they strip you down?" She looked up at him through her lashes as he moved to the music and shifted her around on the dance floor.

"It helps to distract the human and focus the dragon females. They are more likely to let their dragon make the decision when their human is fascinated and aroused."

She felt a blush heating her cheeks,

and she looked down but then was faced with all that tanned muscle and her gaze went up again.

He grinned. "See? Someone once suggested that the women be attired in a similar manner, but the one experiment didn't go anywhere until the ladies were willing to come out from behind the drapes."

She sighed and found herself staring at the thick column of his neck as they moved around the other dancers.

Trin checked on her friends and smiled. Torm was teaching Meadra how to dance on one side of the dance floor, away from the others, and Apraxa and Romak were moving with the fluid grace of those who breathed water. They were fine.

"Did you have any trouble getting

here tonight?"

Trin glanced up at him and smiled. "Vasic's government-issued vehicle was vandalized, and the bartender here tried to drug us."

Brommin tried to get out of her embrace to kill someone, but she held on. "It is fine. I smelled it, and I am guessing that it was a family connection that forced him into this action."

"He is going to be interrogated for that slight."

She nodded. "Yes, Brommin, but not tonight. Tonight is just you and me and the music."

He pulled her tightly against him, and she could feel the outline of his thighs through the silk that he was wearing.

She giggled at the physical hint that

there was more than just the silk between them. "Ah. I see."

"Yes, I am guessing that I am not the only one in this situation, but the others are too polite to do anything about it."

She smiled. "You know what I like about you, Archivist?"

"What?"

"You can dispense with politeness when necessary."

Her permission was in her gaze, and she laughed as his arms came around her and his wings sprouted. He swung her up into his arms, and his heavy wingbeats took them out of the ballroom and up the stairwell.

He carried her past the guards in the hall and to one of the doors that had been propped open.

"That is convenient." She smiled, and

he kicked the doorstop aside before reaching out and latching the manual lock.

"I believe so. Would you like a breakdown on the etiquette of what we are going to do?"

She wrinkled her nose. "I think I have it figured out, and it has something to do with why we are not allowed undergarments with these gowns."

His expression darkened, and he drew his hand up the back of her thigh. He let his breath out slowly. "That is... why do you have a corset on?"

Trin laughed. "I have had a few attempts on my life and Meadra's custody. Mirbella wanted me armed, so I am covered with a number of weapons. Would you like me to show you or can we get into the interesting part?"

He pulled her in close as his fingers worked at the laces of her corset. She gasped when cool air rushed in against sweaty skin. "I think that we can do both."

Her giggles lasted far longer than they should have, and it was only when there was no breath for laughter that she focused on the man she was with. Her mate. It was so much better than the romances she had read as a teen.

* * * *

Apraxa watched Brommin fly off with Trin as she danced with Romak. "It seems they couldn't wait."

She swayed and crossed her right and left feet before returning to his arms.

"They are fliers. They do not appreciate the pleasures of waiting."

She gave him a look through her lashes. "I seem to recall you catching me in a hallway and pressing me up against the wall a few years ago."

"I was young and had no patience for the waiting game."

Apraxa nodded. "You tell yourself that a lot, don't you?"

He leaned down and hissed in her ear, "Yes."

She grinned. "You know there is no reason to wait, right? According to the laws of our people and the senate, we are the next thing to wed. A formal ceremony is all we need for the final documentation, and that is just so that any children I bear will have your name."

The mention of children made him

shudder, and he paused in their intricate dance. "That was cruel."

She went up on her toes and licked the lobe of his pointed ear. "Why was it cruel? The only one keeping us on this dance floor is you."

He grabbed her and strode off to the hall, heading up to the rooms that were set aside for them.

Imagine Apraxa's delight when the tub was large enough to hold six people. The environment was ideal for her first night with her mate.

* * * *

Meadra focused on the steps, but she still ended up stepping on Torm's feet.

He stopped them and kissed her slowly. She went up on her toes and followed him as he leaned back. He smiled against her lips.

Torm wrapped an arm around her waist and held her while they kissed, and when Meadra lifted her head, they were on their circuit around the room. All she had to do was leave her focus behind and trust him. Once she managed that, the rest was easy.

She glanced around, and more than half of the couples were gone. "Where did they go?"

"I imagine that they are making use of the hotel's amenities." Torm kept waltzing.

"Oh. Oh!" She blushed as she caught on. "Right. Of course. Should we go?"

"No. Not until you are comfortable touching me. That is part of the reason for the uniform we are dressed in. It gives you the advantage to learn what your mate feels like."

"You feel like mine." She smiled and ran her hands over his chest, down his abdomen, and around his waist to hold him tight.

His shudder was all self-control, and she fought a smirk. She had been around farm animals all her life. Sex was no great mystery, but knowing that he wanted to ease her into the idea was rather sweet. She was going to have to stop that immediately.

"Torm, I understand that you want to behave in a decorous manner, but do remember that my family could come after me or send someone at any time. My image was in all the evening news media. It would be better for both of us if we could confirm our connection."

He blinked. "You would like to..."

"Seek privacy. With you. Lots of privacy and more kissing, perhaps tangled limbs—" She squeaked on the last words, but he had heard enough. He gathered her up, sprouted his wings and took them up and out of the ballroom.

Torm still had plenty of self-control, but he used it on his own body to the satisfaction of them both.

Chapter Twelve

Getting everyone back to Creata's for a change of clothing had been a bit of effort. Trin smiled at her friend and gave her a hug the moment that Brommin touched down.

"Well. That was an interesting night, and now, I know why there is a non-disclosure agreement." Trin blushed. "I think you can figure out most of it."

The men had tunics delivered to them, so Brommin looked practically normal with comfortable trousers.

He kissed her softly and whispered, "I will pick you up this afternoon. Senator Weekon has already been in touch."

She nodded. "I will be dressed and ready."

Creata was smiling as Brommin left. "So, you have your mate."

Trin blushed. "I am going to get breakfast first. After a shower."

"Good, I can smell him on you from last night."

Trin headed up to her room and called out, "That was from this morning."

* * * *

Meadra had seen Apraxa head upstairs while on a business call, so now, she was staring at her host. "I think I should change as well."

Creata smiled. "I think you should.

Those gowns don't leave anything to the imagination."

Meadra nodded. Torm had dropped her off, given her a short kiss, and left her, murmuring that he had things to do. She didn't know when she would see him again, but they were mated now, so she had legal recourse.

He had been so focused, so tender last night, that now she was completely knocked off her feet by being left like a sack of potatoes.

She headed up to her room and quickly changed. She had showered in the morning, and Torm had simply gotten dressed and waited for her.

To boost her spirits, she put on one of the outfits that had been made expressly for her. She loved Trin's taste in clothing, but it was time to figure out what she wanted. This dress was nearly there. It was easy to move in, fit over her corset and undergarments without too much difficulty, and it was a brilliant amethyst with silver piping. Her new hair colour nearly matched the gown, and it didn't look quite right, but it was hers.

She headed down to meet with Creata and try to make sense of Torm's actions.

* * * *

Trin headed downstairs, and she saw something that filled her with horror. Meadra was crying.

"What is it? What did he do?"

Meadra sniffled and blew her nose delicately into one of Creata's handkerchiefs. "It's Torm. He dropped me off and said he had things to do but didn't say anything else. He just left."

Trin scowled. "That sounds rather rude."

"I don't know what happened. He was fine last night, he held me all night, but when we woke up, he was all determined, but he wouldn't tell me what was going on."

Trin blinked and nodded. "Right. I don't think there is any problem."

Meadra sniffled. "Really?"

"Really. If you don't hear from him by tonight, I will find him and find out why."

"Thank you, Trin. I don't want to be a burden, but this caught me off guard."

Creata nodded. "It would do that to anyone after a mating night. If Vasic had acted that way, Esty might never have become a reality. I would have neutered him."

They laughed together and ate a lot of heavily sweetened pastries.

Apraxa came down, and she was frowning.

Trin groaned. "Not you, too."

"My brothers saw the picture on an online post. They are furious that I kept this from them, and more than that, they want to meet Romak. Now."

Trin sighed. "It sounds like we are scattering."

Creata grinned. "That is life. We come together, we ease apart, but we never forget when we were interlinked."

Trin blinked and smiled. "I see that the counsellor is working."

Creata made a face. She paused and

looked at Meadra. "He didn't say anything, and then, he left. I think I know where he is going and what he is doing."

They all looked at her while waiting. Finally, Meadra said, "What? What is he doing?"

"He has to get his family's engagement ring. He is the oldest son, so he has to go to the family seat and retrieve the ring from his parents. That might not go smoothly, or there may be no problem. He won't know until he gets there."

Meadra blinked. "Really?"

Trin muttered. "I hope so. There is about to be a rash of pregnancies in the dragon world."

Three surprised faces turned to her.

Apraxa whispered, "What?"

"It is a side effect. When my dragon is happy, she spreads the fertility energy around." Trin coughed. "I was happy a few times last night."

It was embarrassing, but it was a fact that she retained from the documents on diamond dragons that she had found.

Meadra and Apraxa put a protective hand over their bellies.

Apraxa bolted to her feet. "I have to make a call."

She left the breakfast area, and Meadra looked down at her hand. "I really hope Creata was right about Torm. If not, I am going to have to work on suing him for breach of contract."

Trin patted her hand. "It won't come to that. Besides, it would be nice not to be the only bastard in the family."

"Not funny."

"A little funny."

Creata snorted. "Don't tease her. Not everyone bounces back like you do."

"I work at it. Hey, I know. Why don't I take you two to one of the shops for a proper high tea? We can meet up with Niida and chat."

Creata sighed. "I have to feed Esty."

"Feed her before we leave and bring her along."

Creata blinked and slowly grinned. "Right. I can do that. I had forgotten."

"So, put on some outside clothing and proper shoes, feed the baby, and we can either go for a walk, or I can fly us all."

Creata bolted from the table and headed upstairs.

Trin smiled. "I think Apraxa is going to find a flight home. If she needs a suggestion, I think I know of one dragon who might just be done with the capitol."

Meadra had flickers of hope in her eyes, and Trin hoped that Creata was right. All Trin could manage was a diversion.

Trin held little Esty for most of the walk. By the time they arrived at the tea shop, they were all hungry again and taking a seat was most welcome.

Niida had brightened when they came through the door. They chose a table with an extra seat, and when she had a moment, she sat with them.

The conversation about the night before had to be kept in low tones. There were interested ears at every table, and some were reading copies of the morning news. Trin's skin had reflected most of the light into a dazzling glow, but Apraxa was clearly a sea creature. In all the flashes, her eyes had gone shark black. Meadra was glittering in the images, and the speculation about who their trio was, was evident.

Trin nibbled at the treats on the tray and relaxed as she was finally able to eat out in public without worry of being poisoned. Sure, the poison probably wouldn't have an effect, but it could injure or kill her friends. Last night's efforts were an example of someone trying to get at her in a safe space, so part of her was going to always remain on guard.

Niida had asked Meadra if anything they spoke of last night had set Torm off.

"He asked me why we were drinking sodas when the guys came in, and I laughingly told him about you stopping the bartender and him apologizing. Torm went quiet after that and kissed my shoulder before holding me until I fell asleep." Meadra looked at Trin. "Could that have been it?"

Trin looked at Creata, and she nodded. "It might have been a contributing factor, but it just means that Torm has to take your welfare more seriously than he thought."

"So, when we woke up..."

"He got moving." Trin sipped at her tea. It was one of the blends she had bought in Breaker City. The light citrus mixed with the green tea in a delightful way.

The door was dropped back into its

frame, and Esty startled, snuffling and wailing softly. She was such a little lady.

The women who had disdainfully dropped the door looked over and sneered at the infant. "What is that doing in here?"

Niida got to her feet, and she spoke firmly. "She is a guest, as you are. How may I help you?"

The ladies appeared to be older dragons. Why they were in the shop was anybody's guess.

"We wish to have tea."

Trin looked around and raised her brows. The shop was full.

"I am sorry, madam. We are full to capacity, and we do not rush our clients. They may remain as long as they wish."

Trin smiled. That was exactly right. The rushing was all done across the hall at the coffee shop.

"You don't understand. We are here for tea, and perhaps that table of your *friends* will make room for us."

Niida stiffened her spine. "No. They are enjoying their time here, and I have no inclination to run them off."

The entire shop was watching the woman, and she had her head high. When she said her next sentence, Creata and Trin mouthed the words with her.

"Do you know who I am?"

Niida cocked her head. "I do not care. You are welcome to return in half an hour when the clients may or may not have completed their socializing."

The woman jerked her chin up and doubled down. "My daughter is the diamond dragon, and she will see this little shop destroyed."

Niida smiled. "Is she? Please. Let her come. I welcome her destruction."

The woman was huffing. "She will be here in a moment, and then, you will see."

Niida inclined her head. "We have waiting chairs near the door. Please be comfortable while you wait."

Trin was fascinated. This was going to be interesting.

A woman with white-blonde hair entered the shop a moment later and stopped still when she saw her mother by the door, along with her mother's two cronies. "I told you to get a table."

Her mother jumped to her feet and went to face Niida again. "She is here. Will you deny her a table?"

Niida cocked her head at the young woman. "You are the diamond dragon?"

The girl snorted fire. "I am, and I will burn this place down around you unless you find us a seat."

Trin got to her feet. "That's it. Please excuse me."

The girl was working up a ball of fire, and Trin reached around to grab it, shoving it back into her throat. The girl squawked, and smoke came out of her nostrils.

The mother was sputtering. "What are you doing? She can destroy us all."

Trin gave the woman a bland look. "She really can't. Crystal fire can work on thermally shocking pottery and scorching hair, but it can't do much to anything else."

Trin turned the girl to face her, and the rage drained from the girl's face.

Trin leaned in and whispered, "I am up for a queen fight, but I don't want to kill anyone on my first day as a bonded mate. Start acting your age, behave, and tell your mother what you actually are, scorched crystal dragon. Oh, and stop bleaching your hair. It is getting all dry and brittle. It is not a good look for a young lady."

The mother was stunned, the cronies looked ill, and the girl burst into tears at having the fiction ripped away.

"Don't play at being me, youngling. I don't like it."

Trin released the girl, who staggered back into her mother's arms. She explained about seeing the dragon at the Wheel, but no one else knew who she was, so it was easy to bleach her hair and call herself the diamond dragon when the identification came out.

The mortified mother still didn't understand, so Trin hardened her skin from head to toe. The four bowed and apologized as they backed out of the shop.

Trin resumed her normal appearance and sat back at the table, sipping at her tea. There were gazes on her from around the room, but it was Creata giving her a thumbs-up that made her relax. This was her city, and she was going to have to learn to live in it as the diamond dragon of the Lefarge family, as soon as Brommin got the paperwork arranged.

Chapter Thirteen

Torm's panicked expression eased as he entered the tea shop and saw Meadra sitting and laughing.

Trin watched the flicker of emotion as it moved through him. It was sweet.

"Meadra, I have looked everywhere for you."

Creata leaned toward Trin and said, "By that, it means he went to my house, and the maids told him where we were."

Torm scowled at her, swallowed, and refocused on Meadra. He went down on one knee and lifted a hand holding a box. "Meadra Anders, will you marry me... today?"

Meadra blinked and looked down at the box. "What is in it?"

He smiled. "Open it."

Meadra opened the box, and she gasped. Inside the small box was a ring with a wide stone in it, marked with a swirl of tiny gems. "It is a constellation."

"It is our family name, the griffon. Will you be Meadra Anders Griffin?"

She smiled and nodded. "I will."

He fumbled a bit as he handled the ring box, but he slid the ring onto her left hand, and he kissed the knuckle above the ring. "Right. Let's go."

He paused and looked at Trin. "With your permission."

"Take her, just know that a formal ceremony will be in your future. I want to give my aunty-mom away."

Meadra grinned, and Torm smiled. He pulled her to her feet, and they headed out of the shop.

Trin turned her head and watched them get into a karros to be delivered to the magistrate or however dragons got married on paper.

"Registry office. That is where they are going. His family is surprisingly up-beat for siring such a scowling and brooding fellow. I think Meadra will be good for him." Brommin spoke from behind Trin.

She whirled. "When did you get here?"

Creata smiled. "When you were watching the proposal. It was so cute. He couldn't believe you didn't see him."

Esty was hoisted up so she could watch what was about to happen.

Brommin smiled, and he went down

on both knees with astonishing grace. His wings grew and flared out behind him.

"Trin Lem, diamond dragon, will you do me the honour of being my wife? My mate? My partner in life?"

She liked that he was addressing both of them. "Brommin Lefarge, obsidian dragon, will you be my husband, my mate, and my partner in life, because I am going to live for a very long time."

He grinned. "I will if you will."

"I will."

He reached behind him and pulled out a long and slender object. He extended it to her on his fingertips.

The object was wrapped in black silk, and she blinked in surprise when she opened it. The blade that was inside the silk was small, but it was studded with a march of faceted stones that wrapped around the hilt.

"You had this made for me."

He smiled. "From the moment I met you I knew that we were going to be together. The family has a ton of jewels, but this is yours and yours alone, as am I."

She carefully folded the knife so that it laid along her skin, and then, she threw her arms around his neck. "Thank you. All I have for you is the next Lefarge."

He paused and his hands wrapped tight around her. "How can you be sure?"

"She's sure, so I am sure. Apparently, it is what diamond dragons do and why we are known to be so benevolent and generous. Fertility goddesses of ancient times. I didn't know it worked on me as well."

"It might have been the zenith." His gaze was analytical.

She chuckled. "So, do we follow Torm and Meadra to the registry office?"

"We will." He looked around at the others at her table. "Are you coming, too?"

Creata grinned. "Is there room?"

He jerked his head at the window, and a long and dark karros was waiting for them. "There is room for you."

Trin smiled. "Niida, you are coming with us. Tlian, you can take over for an hour or two."

Tlian gave her a salute. "Congratulations."

Niida nodded and took out her communicator. "I am calling Brenner."

By the time they were all in the vehi-

cle, Brenner was on his way, Vasic was leaving his office for the day.

Even though it was a civil ceremony, folk were coming in from around the city. Even Apraxa and her mate were delaying their departure so that they could attend. Brommin was assigning them a dragon to fly them to Breaker City by nightfall, taking them away right after the ceremony.

Trin sat next to Brommin, her new blade tucked into a sheath in her corset. Their vehicle was driving at a stately pace, and Creata was doing a quick feeding of Esty, so she wasn't going to be fussing during the ceremony.

The tea shop had been buzzing with laughter and congratulations when they left, and by now, the word was all over the city.

Trin put it out of her mind and leaned her head against Brommin's shoulder. She already knew his parents, and if his siblings were anything like him, she would fit in just fine.

She had found one family by circumstance, one by accident, and now, she was finding another by saying words in front of witnesses. In less than a year she would start her own. So many routes to family and she knew there were more she hadn't even explored.

The crowd gathered around the registry office was getting larger with every passing second.

Trin cleared her throat. "That can't be for us."

"I believe it is, Trin. Come on, let's run escort for our guests."

She nodded and brought her wings out the moment she was out of the vehicle. Creata and the baby were tucked under one wing, Niida under the other. Brenner came out of the gathered horde, and Brommin covered him. Apraxa and Romak made their own way through the crowd.

Their group converged and entered the registry office where guards were at the door with wide eyes.

Brommin spoke quickly, and they were allowed in.

Inside, she pulled her wings in but folded them along her back.

Meadra and Torm were still at the office.

"Why are you here?"

"After last night, there was a rash of legal marriages. We are next." Torm smiled.

Brommin grinned. "I had better get in line then."

Trin nodded. "We will just do what

we have to, but if you want witnesses, you have plenty to choose from."

Meadra grinned. "I can see that."

Trin and Brommin went to fill out the registry paperwork, but it had already been done. Trin was suspicious. "How is that possible?"

Brommin chuckled. "Dr. Dredock works on the bloodwork to make sure that no apocalypse dragons are born. She would have filled out the paperwork the minute that the selection was done last night."

Apraxa asked from behind them, "So, is our stuff in there as well?"

Brommin waited until their file was put in line for the magistrate, and he waved Apraxa forward. Her paperwork was done already, so she would be in after they were.

Meadra called out, "We are going in, come on!"

The gathering of folk in the hallway surged into the office and divided along the bride's and groom's sides. The bemused magistrate looked at the North American senator standing on the groom's side, and he nodded. "Right. Okay."

Creata was standing with Meadra, and to her amusement, so was Vasic. Vasic was holding his daughter and bouncing her gently.

Torm was surrounded by those who had been raised at or lived in the capitol, including Brommin.

The magistrate straightened his paperwork. "Right. Torm, Meadra, please stand in front of me."

They stepped forward.

Trin watched them say their vows, and Meadra turned to her when a witness was called for. Trin stepped forward and signed her official name for the second to last time.

Trin signed with a flourish and handed the pen off to the next witness, Senator Lefarge.

She gave Meadra a hug and congratulated Torm with a handshake the moment that they parted after the magistrate's announcement that they could kiss.

The magistrate cleared his throat. "If you could all clear the room for the next couple?"

Trin and Brommin stepped forward. "We are here."

The magistrate noted that no one left the room. "Right. Okay. Well, Adolla Venatrin Lem and Brommin Artur Lefarge, please step forward."

Trin and Brommin smiled.

"I have been given special instructions by the senator for this registration. Just a moment." He picked up a piece of heavy parchment and raised his brows. "Right. Okay. Well, Adolla, who gives you in marriage to this dragon?"

A raucous shout from behind her sounded, "We do."

She whirled, and her friends were all there, including Mirbella. They were all smiling and laughing.

The magistrate continued, "Brommin, who gives you in marriage to this dragon?"

"We do!" His family roared to outdo Trin's side, but theirs didn't have a wailing baby for emotional impact.

The magistrate got down to business. "Trin, do you?"

"I do."

"Brommin, do you?"

"I do."

"You may now kiss the groom." The magistrate tapped the page in front of him.

Trin wrapped her arms around his neck and kissed him soundly. He twisted her and dipped her so that her wings were across his knee and their friends and family were getting a very good view.

He pulled her upright and released her. The magistrate remembered that they hadn't signed anything, and they ended up signing after the kiss, which meant another kiss. Brenner was her witness, and Rish signed for Brommin.

They moved back into the crowd as Apraxa and Romak stepped up. Their ceremony was surrounded by those who wished them nothing but the best, and when they called for witnesses, Meadra was called, as was the sea dragon who had not found a mate, Temmor.

Their kiss was more formal but no less heated than the ones that had preceded it.

The magistrate looked rather relieved when they all filed out.

Rish came up to them and smiled. "Congratulations. We are having your clothing from the tower sent to our country home, and we will send someone to Creata's to do the same."

Creata was smiling softly. "It's okay, Trin. The sleepover couldn't last forever, but now that you are mated, you will be closer to home."

"I won't need to run, that is certain." Trin smiled.

Vasic came up to her and hugged her. "Thank you for being Creata's friend and Esty's godmother."

"It has been fun, and I have an entire chest of baby items for her that should be arriving in the next few days."

Vasic rolled his eyes. "Small tools?"

Trin clapped him on the shoulder. "You wish."

Brommin wrapped his arm around her. "There is a huge crowd. I think we should head to the family estate via the roof."

"Got it. Full form?"

He looked impressed. "Can you change in mid-flight?"

"I have to, I am too damned big to launch off this roof."

Brommin chuckled. "I love every inch of you, my bride."

She blinked. "Huh. I guess I am that, husband."

There was a visible shiver that went

through him. "Right. Let's go."

They moved through the crowd inside the building and headed for the roof. If the folks from the Delarm Valley tried to make a claim on Meadra, they couldn't. She was pregnant and married. That broke all ties to her family. It was as safe as Trin could have made her without burning the valley to the ground.

The light that streamed in when they opened the roof door was welcome to her gaze.

She let out a happy shout, flared her wings, and propelled herself off the roof, climbing upward with wide wingbeats. When she was high enough, she let her dragon free and glided until the change was complete, using her wings to keep her gently aloft until her body and wingspan were balanced once again.

Brommin changed into his magnificent and faceted obsidian dragon. His fire could melt stone and carve through the earth. The edges of his wings could slice as easily as hers if it came to it. They were a match, and they were flying.

Trin paused in midair. She had no idea where they were going.

Brommin's dragon laughed and led the way. He knew where she needed to be, and she trusted him enough to follow him today. Tomorrow would be its own situation.

As they flew, she idly wondered how many types of family she could experience in her lifetime. She was already at four—soon to be five—perhaps more were lurking around the corner.

Mirbella smiled from inside the crowd and watched the two dragons flying for a bit of privacy.

It was so nice that the first of the prophecies had come to pass in her lifetime. She was going to have to write to her cousin in Rekker City and find out if there were any signs of the new dragon who was supposed to be appearing there.

The diamond dragon was the first sign. The world as they knew it was about to undergo a powerful change, and watching it was what Mirbella lived for.

Whew. So, ends Trin's arc. I thought it was going to be a short little trilogy, but I don't know myself very well.

Dragon Undone will see us in Rekker City, where Councillor Kreelo is from. It is a city of humans and wizards with the dragons in charge to keep anything from going cataclysmic.

Aeli is our main character, and she has a huge chip on her shoulder. Her father was kicked off the wizard council, and their shop was cursed before she was born. The insult to her family honour must be avenged, and getting the dragons out of Rekker City is her primary priority.

I hope to release it in March 2019

Thanks for reading,

Viola Grace

About the Author

Viola Grace (aka Zenina Masters) is a Canadian sci-fi/paranormal romance writer with ambitions to keep writing for the rest of her life. She specializes in short stories because the thrill of discovery, of all those firsts, is what keeps her writing.

An artist who enjoys a story that catches you up, whirls you around, and sets you down with a smile on your face is all she endeavours to be. She prefers to leave the drama to those who are better suited to it, she always goes for the cheap laugh.

In real life, she now is engaged in beekeeping, and her adventures can be found on the YouTube channel, Mystery Bees Apiary. Just look for the cartoon kittens.